POWER PACK™

AF825680

Origin Album

Published by Marvel Comics Group, a New World Company.
387 Park Avenue South, New York, New York 10016

Manufactured in the United States of America

ISBN 0-87135-385-7

Louise Simonson
script/co-creator
June Brigman
penciler/co-creator
Bob Wiacek
inker
Joe Rosen
letterer
Glynis Wein
colors
Marc McLaurin
assistant editor
Carl Potts
editor
Tom DeFalco
editor in chief
Cindy Kruhm
Marc McLaurin
Design

I'm often asked, "How did you get the idea for a group of kid super-heroes? Where did Power Pack come from?"

The answer is . . . from lots of places.

Alex, Julie, Jack and Katie are the lineal descendants of Jane, Mark, Katherine and Martha from Edward Eager's wonderful *Half Magic* (who owed their existence to E. Nesbit's magical children); of Meg, Jo, Beth, Amy and Laurie of Louisa May Alcott's *Little Women*; of Kip Russell and Peewee of Robert Heinlein's *Have Space Suit — Will Travel*. Power Pack owe, of course, a huge debt to Stan Lee and Steve Ditko's *Spider-Man*.

These fictional kids generally faced life's difficulties with intelligence, creativity, courage, humor and flexibility. They were also fallible, human characters and came with a comforting array of faults. They were the heroes who led the way.

The kids of Power Pack are a synthesis of mine and June Brigman's creative vision. It was easy for me to imagine a grumpy little eight-year-old who could control the density of his body. But June's initial sketch, the stance, the pout . . . shaped Jack Power's character as much as my more abstract imaginings. That boy that she drew became Jack Power, the incredible Mass Master. So was it with them all.

When the alien Aelfyre Whitemane crashed into the Power kids' lives, he gave them special gifts based on energy, density, velocity and gravity and the opportunity to save their world. That's a lot to ask of a bunch of kids who aren't in high school yet.

How a person, real or fictional, meets a challenge defines who he or she is. The Power Pack kids always met the challenge. It made them real for me . . . and a lot of people who follow their continuing adventures. They're super kids in every way.

LOUISE SIMONSON
February, 1988

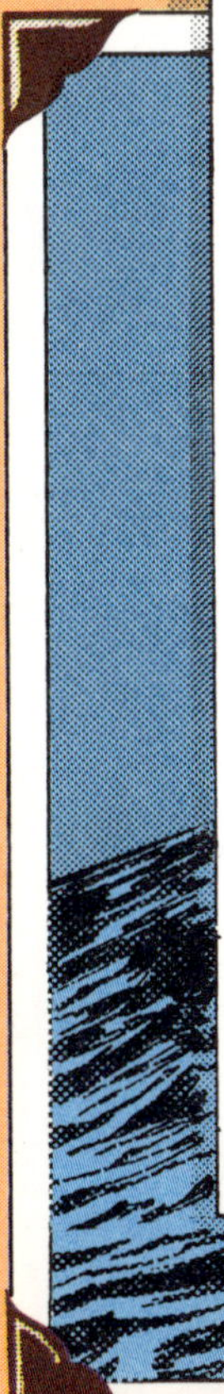

POWER PLAY
LOUISE SIMONSON JUNE BRIGMAN
SCRIPT- CREATORS- PENCILLER
BOB WIACEK INKER
JOE ROSEN LETTERER
GLYNIS WEIN COLORS
CARL POTTS EDITOR
JIM SHOOTER EDITOR-IN-CHIEF
SNARK FIGHTERS-- AND A STARCRUISER! FRIDAY, WHAT ARE *THEY* DOING HERE?
ATTACKING US AT PRESENT. NO DOUBT WE SHARE THE SAME OBJECTIVE. BUT REMEMBER, WHITEY, *HE WHO FIGHTS AND RUNS AWAY LIVES TO FIGHT ANOTHER DAY.*
A COWARDLY ALTERNATIVE FOR WHICH *YOU* PRUDENTLY PROGRAMMED ME. WE ARE INSUFFICIENTLY ARMED AND EARTH IS RIGHT BELOW.
THAT ONE WAS CLOSE! FRIDAY, IT IS A BIT LATE TO ASK, BUT ARE YOU *CERTAIN* THAT DR. POWER HAS DISCOVERED THE ANNIHILATION EFFECT?
I HAVE RECHECKED HIS FORMULA. NOT ONLY HAS HE DISCOVERED IT--HE HAS BUILT A DEVICE TO TEST IT...
...AND IF HE DOES, HE COULD UNKNOWINGLY SET OFF A CHAIN REACTION THAT WILL DESTROY HIS WORLD!
SKRA-KKOW

MEANWHILE...
HE SWINGS! IT'S A LONG FLY BALL TO RIGHT CENTER. IT'S IN THERE!
HOLY COW--IT'S INTO THE RIGHT FIELD BLEACHERS!
WAHOOO! A HOMER!
HEY, THAT GLASS YOU'RE TOSSING AROUND IS SPLASHING WATER ALL OVER MY BOOK!
YEAH--SHAPE UP, JACK! BE CAREFUL OR YOU'LL SMASH IT!
YOU BE CAREFUL, MISTER SMART-ALEX...
...OR I'LL SMASH THAT PRECIOUS TELESCOPE YOU'RE BUILDING!
CUT IT OUT, YOU TWO! MIND YOUR OWN BUSINESS, ALEX. JACK, KEEP DRYING! IT LOOKS LIKE JULIE'S GETTING WAY AHEAD OF YOU...
...THOUGH HOW ANYONE CAN WASH DISHES AND READ AT THE SAME TIME IS BEYOND ME!

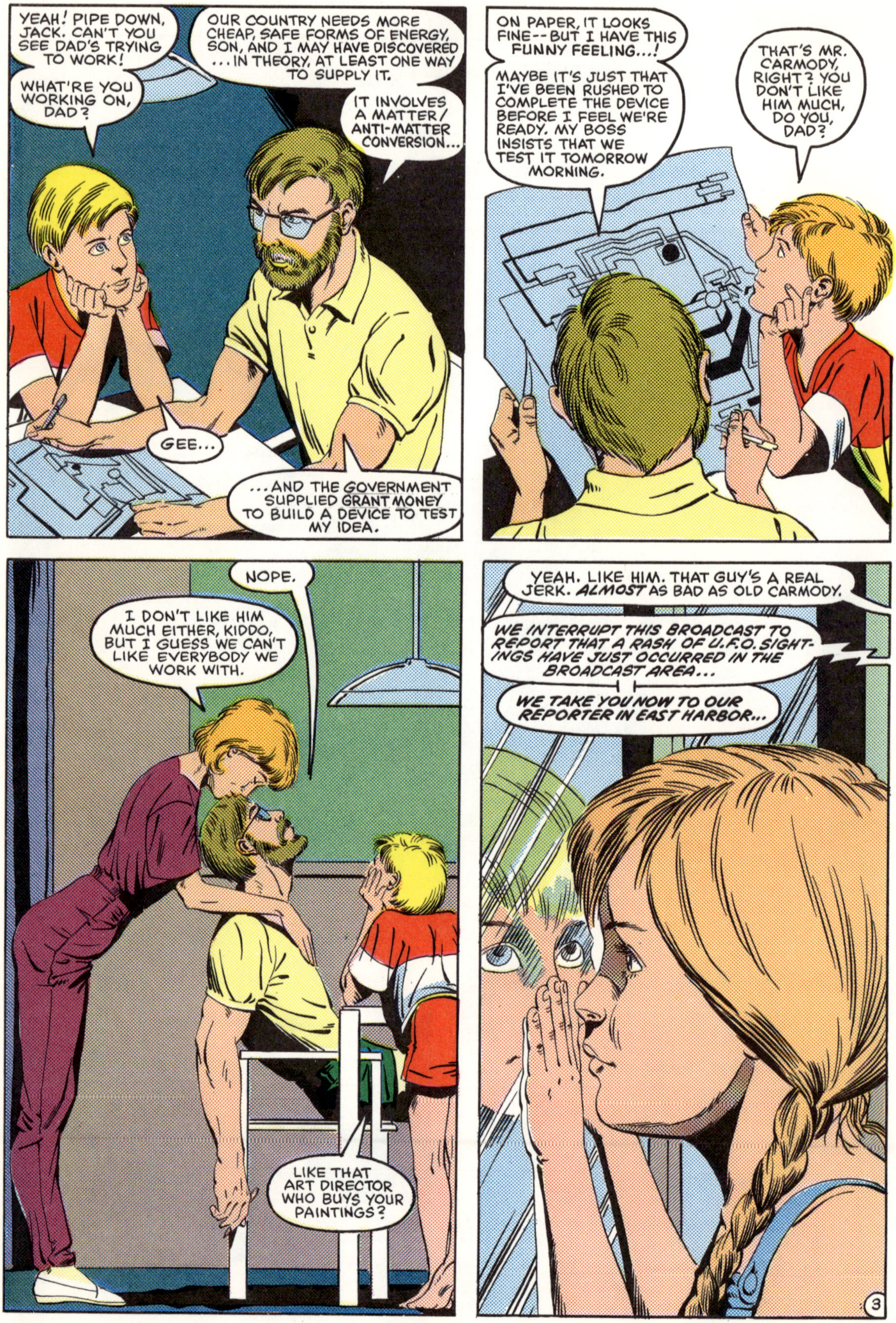
YEAH! PIPE DOWN, JACK. CAN'T YOU SEE DAD'S TRYING TO WORK!
WHAT'RE YOU WORKING ON, DAD?
OUR COUNTRY NEEDS MORE CHEAP, SAFE FORMS OF ENERGY, SON, AND I MAY HAVE DISCOVERED ...IN THEORY, AT LEAST ONE WAY TO SUPPLY IT.
IT INVOLVES A MATTER/ ANTI-MATTER CONVERSION...
GEE...
...AND THE GOVERNMENT SUPPLIED GRANT MONEY TO BUILD A DEVICE TO TEST MY IDEA.
ON PAPER, IT LOOKS FINE--BUT I HAVE THIS FUNNY FEELING...!
MAYBE IT'S JUST THAT I'VE BEEN RUSHED TO COMPLETE THE DEVICE BEFORE I FEEL WE'RE READY. MY BOSS INSISTS THAT WE TEST IT TOMORROW MORNING.
THAT'S MR. CARMODY, RIGHT? YOU DON'T LIKE HIM MUCH, DO YOU, DAD?
NOPE.
I DON'T LIKE HIM MUCH EITHER, KIDDO, BUT I GUESS WE CAN'T LIKE EVERYBODY WE WORK WITH.
LIKE THAT ART DIRECTOR WHO BUYS YOUR PAINTINGS?
YEAH. LIKE HIM. THAT GUY'S A REAL JERK. ALMOST AS BAD AS OLD CARMODY.
WE INTERRUPT THIS BROADCAST TO REPORT THAT A RASH OF U.F.O. SIGHTINGS HAVE JUST OCCURRED IN THE BROADCAST AREA...
WE TAKE YOU NOW TO OUR REPORTER IN EAST HARBOR...

WHILE ABOVE...
THE SNARKS MUST HAVE INTERCEPTED AND JAMMED OUR TRANS-MISSIONS HOME.
YES. IT APPEARS WE ARE ON OUR OWN.
WE CAME HERE TO STUDY THE HUMANS, FRIDAY! NOT TO PLACE THE ENTIRE GALAXY IN JEOPARDY!
WE DID NOT DISCOVER THIS FORMULA!
BUT THE SNARKS LEARNED OF IT THROUGH US.
PERHAPS THEY WILL USE IT IN THEIR OWN INTERNAL CONFLICTS ...TO LAY WASTE TO THEIR GALAXY ALONE!
AT FIRST, PERHAPS. EVENTU-ALLY THEY WILL TURN IT UPON OTHERS. AND THE RE-SULT WILL BE TOO TERRIBLE TO CONTEMPLATE.
SO FAR WE KNOW THE HUMANS ONLY THROUGH THEIR TRANS-MISSIONS AND THE LITERATURE STORED IN THEIR COMPU-TER BANKS...
...BUT A PLANET'S WRITINGS SHOW WHAT ITS PEOPLE ASPIRE TO. AND WE CANNOT ALLOW THOSE WHO GAVE US "ALICE IN WONDERLAND" TO BE DESTROYED.
WHY, YOU CHOSE YOUR NAME FROM ONE OF THEIR HEROES! YOU LOVE THESE PEOPLE AS MUCH AS I DO!
WILL YOU LOVE THEM AS MUCH WHEN YOU ARE FORCED TO DIE FOR THEM?
WHITEY...?
YES?
I DO NOT WANT YOU TO DIE.
I LOVE YOU TOO, FRIDAY!
BA-DOOM!
THERE'S OUR TARGET! WE'RE GOING DOWN!
FRIDAY! CAN YOU WIPE THE FORMULA FROM DR. POWER'S EARTH COMPUTERS? IF WE CAN TAP INTO THEM, SO CAN THE SNARKS!
SURE.

WE RETURN YOU NOW TO OUR GAME IN PROGRESS.
AW, GOOD GRIEF! THEY INTERRUPTED THE BASEBALL GAME FOR THAT?
U.F.O.'S ARE JUST SCIENCE FICTION... LIKE THE STUFF IN THOSE BOOKS MOM PAINTS THE COVERS FOR. THERE'S REALLY NO SUCH THING!
I'LL BET THERE IS, TOO!
SCIENCE FICTION ALWAYS COMES TRUE EVENTUALLY...
...LIKE JULES VERNE. HE WROTE ABOUT SUBMARINES... AND THEN SOMEBODY INVENTED THEM.
I'LL BET SOMEBODY EVEN WROTE A BOOK ABOUT DAD'S INVENTION... RIGHT, DAD?
OH, WOW!
MOM! EVERYBODY! THERE ARE U.F.O.S!
IT IS TRUE! I SAW THEM IN THE SKY!
CRASH!
SPLASH!
MY BOOK!

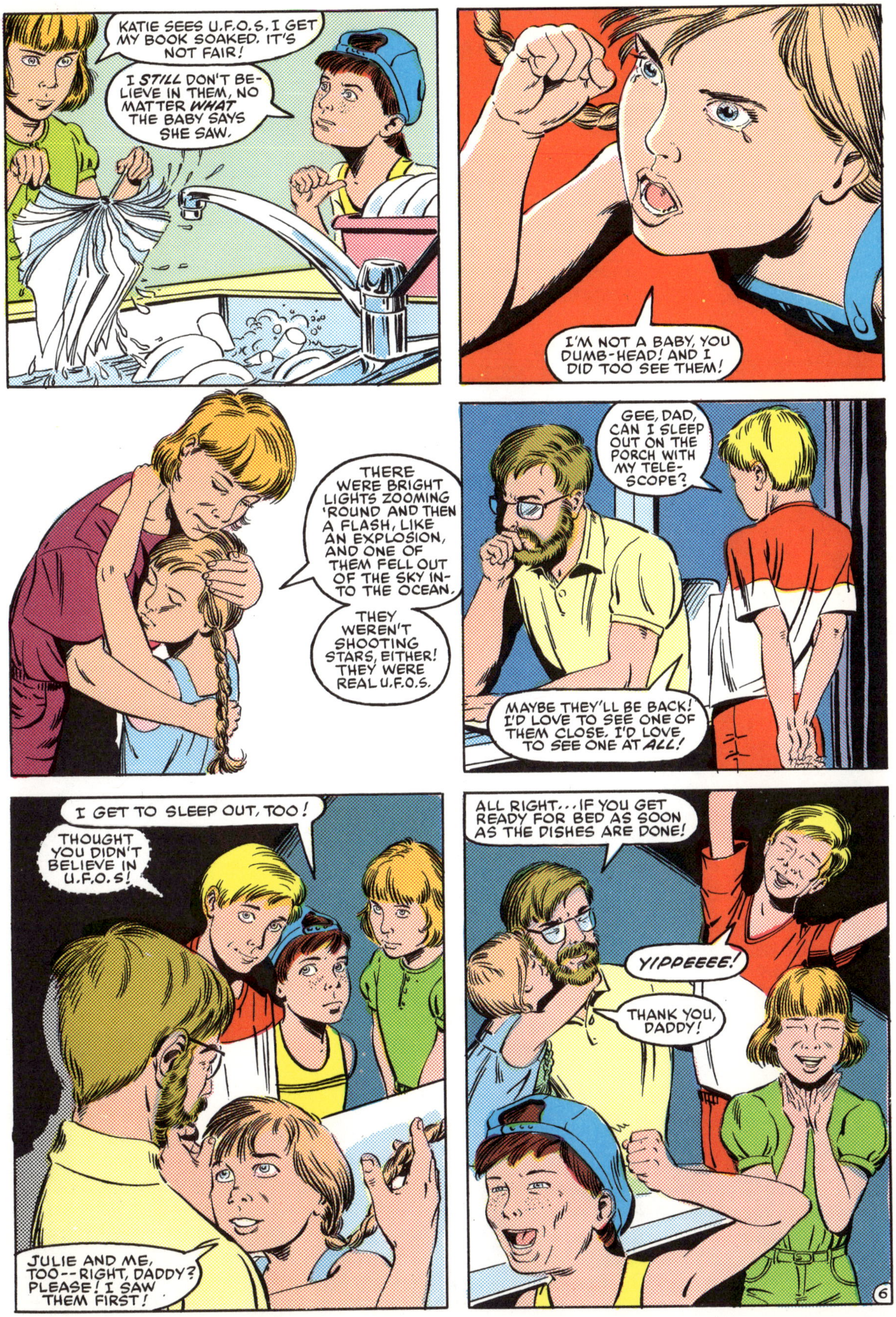

KATIE SEES U.F.O.S. I GET MY BOOK SOAKED. IT'S NOT FAIR!
I STILL DON'T BELIEVE IN THEM, NO MATTER WHAT THE BABY SAYS SHE SAW.
I'M NOT A BABY, YOU DUMB-HEAD! AND I DID TOO SEE THEM!
THERE WERE BRIGHT LIGHTS ZOOMING 'ROUND AND THEN A FLASH, LIKE AN EXPLOSION, AND ONE OF THEM FELL OUT OF THE SKY INTO THE OCEAN.
THEY WEREN'T SHOOTING STARS, EITHER! THEY WERE REAL U.F.O.S.
GEE, DAD, CAN I SLEEP OUT ON THE PORCH WITH MY TELESCOPE?
MAYBE THEY'LL BE BACK! I'D LOVE TO SEE ONE OF THEM CLOSE. I'D LOVE TO SEE ONE AT ALL!
I GET TO SLEEP OUT, TOO!
THOUGHT YOU DIDN'T BELIEVE IN U.F.O.S!
JULIE AND ME, TOO--RIGHT, DADDY? PLEASE! I SAW THEM FIRST!
ALL RIGHT... IF YOU GET READY FOR BED AS SOON AS THE DISHES ARE DONE!
YIPPEEEE!
THANK YOU, DADDY!

HOURS LATER, ALEX'S TELESCOPE STILL POINTS AT THE EMPTY SKY, LONG AFTER THE WATCHER HAS ABANDONED HIS POST...
HUH--WHAT IS THAT?
OH! JULIE'S FLASHLIGHT'S SHINING IN MY EYES. SHE MUST HAVE FALLEN ASLEEP READING.
FOR A MINUTE I THOUGHT IT WAS A U.F.O.
DADDY'S GONNA LECTURE HER ABOUT WASTING THE BATTERIES AGAIN, I'LL BET.
CLIK!
THERE'S SOMETHING OUT THERE!
IT MUST HAVE WASHED IN ON THE TIDE!
I CAN'T TELL WHAT IT IS THOUGH.

I KNOW-- ALEX'S *TELESCOPE!*
I'LL BE ABLE TO SEE IT REAL GOOD THROUGH *THAT!*
CRASH!
KATIE!
ALEX TOLD YOU NOT TO TOUCH THAT! IF YOU'VE CRACKED THE LENS--
I DIDN'T! HONEST! I JUST WANTED TO SEE!
THERE'S A GLOWING THING DOWN THERE -- ON THE BEACH!
A GLOWING THING?
THERE *IS* SOMETHING THERE.
YEAH! BUT *WHAT?*
I CAN'T TELL, BUT IT'S WEIRD!
MAYBE IT'S A U.F.O.!
8

THERE'S NO SUCH THING, SCAREDY-BABY! LET'S GO DOWN AND CHECK IT OUT AND I'LL PROVE IT!
I'M NOT AFRAID! IT'S JUST THAT...
MAYBE KATIE'S RIGHT, JACK. MAYBE WE SHOULD TELL DAD!
CHICKEN!
LOOK, IF WE TELL DAD, BY THE TIME HE GETS READY, THE TIDE'LL HAVE TURNED AND WASHED IT OUT TO SEA.
WE'LL NEVER FIND OUT WHAT IT WAS.
I GUESS YOU'RE RIGHT! OKAY, LET'S GO!
YOU COMING, JULIE?
U.F.O.S ON OUR BEACH! THIS IS SCAREY--BUT IT'S FUN TOO! LIKE PLAYING PRETEND...ONLY THIS IS REAL!
YEAH, I'M COMING TOO!
DON'T BE AFRAID, KATIE. I'LL HOLD YOUR HAND!
AND THE FOUR CHILDREN RUN DOWN TO THE BEACH AND THE BRIGHT THING BOBBING ON THE TIDE.

OH... WOW!
IT'S KATIE'S U.F.O.! IT'S REAL!
I WONDER IF ANYBODY'S IN THERE.
SURE SOMEBODY'S IN THERE-- ALIENS OF SOME KIND. IT DIDN'T FLY HERE BY ITSELF!
KATIE SAW AN EXPLOSION! MAYBE THEY WERE KILLED! IT IS AWFULLY QUIET!
WHAT IF MONSTERS ARE INSIDE? WE OUGHTA GO GET DAD!
WE COULD KNOCK!
DON'T!
KNOCK KNOCK
IS ANYBODY HOME?
NO ANSWER ...I'LL BET THEY ARE DEAD!
NO! THEY CAN'T BE!
I WANT TO GO BACK TO THE HOUSE, ALEX! I'M SCARED!
I'M NOT! MOVE! I WANT TO LOOK THROUGH THE GLASS!

HOLY COW! I THINK I SEE SOMEBODY ONLY THEY'RE NOT MOVING.
I CAN'T QUITE MAKE THEM OUT. IT'S TOO SMOKEY. TAKE A LOOK!
GEE, YOU'RE RIGHT. WE'D BETTER GET DAD.
I'LL WAIT HERE. YOU THREE HEAD BACK TO THE HOUSE...AND TRY TO MAKE DAD HURRY!
IT'S MY U.F.O.! I SAW IT FIRST! I'M NOT LEAVING IT AND YOU CAN'T MAKE ME!
PLEASE LET ME STAY WITH YOU, ALEX! PLEEEASE!
WE'LL WASTE MORE TIME ARGUING WITH HER THAN IT'S WORTH.
DOESN'T ANYBODY EVER SAY NO TO THIS KID?
OH, LET HER STAY, ALEX. YOU'LL BE HERE TO LOOK AFTER HER...
...AND JACK AND I CAN REACH DAD FASTER ALONE!
11

MOM! DAD!
COME QUICK--
HOLY COW!
RRRRRRMMMMM
ANOTHER U.F.O.-- A GIANT ONE!
DO YOU SEE, JACK? THE VIBRATIONS FROM IT ARE SHAKING OUR HOUSE!
WE'VE GOT TO HIDE!
WE CAN'T, JULIE! MOM AND DAD ARE IN THERE! WE'VE GOT TO SAVE THEM!

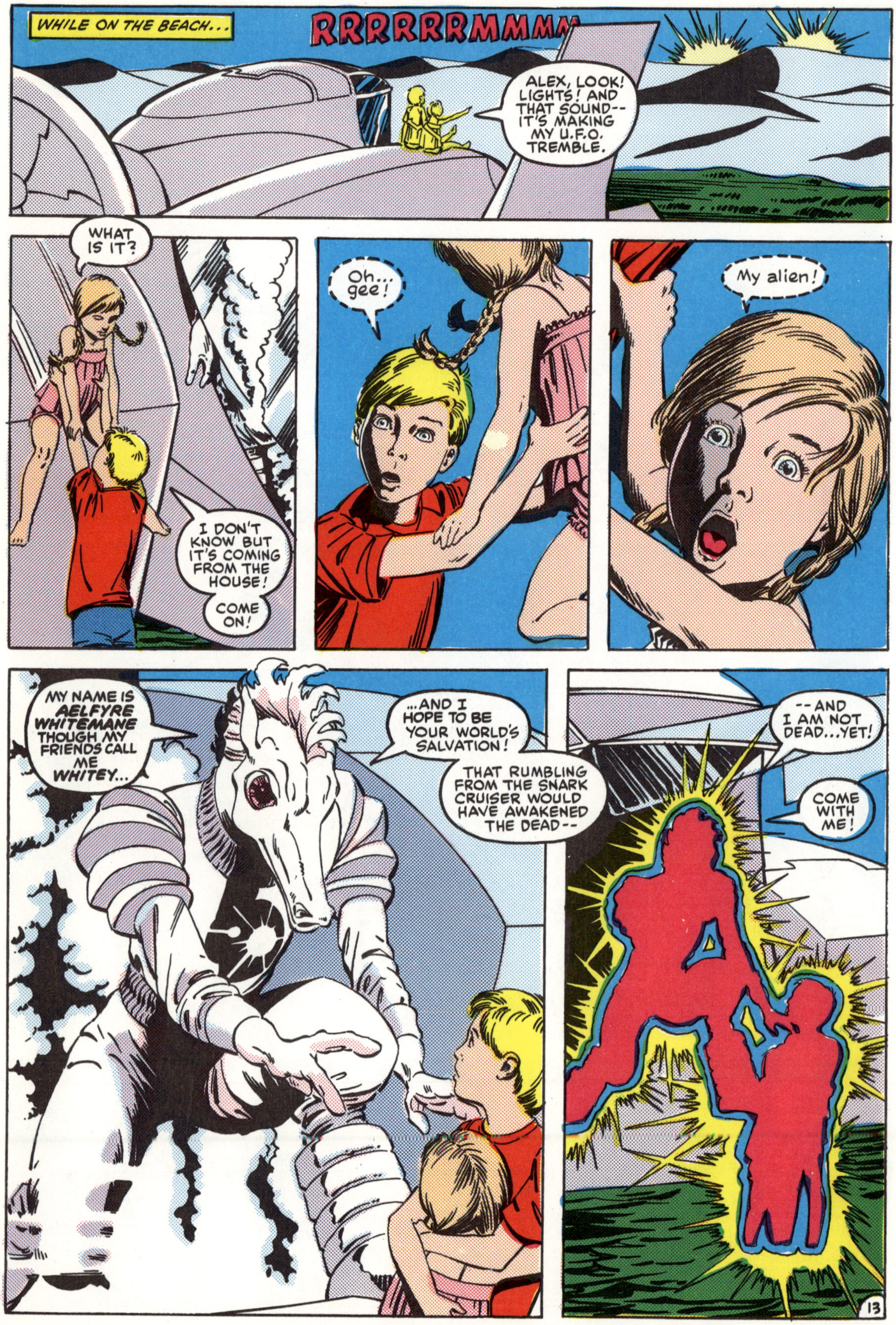
WHILE ON THE BEACH...
RRRRRRMMMM
ALEX, LOOK! LIGHTS! AND THAT SOUND-- IT'S MAKING MY U.F.O. TREMBLE.
WHAT IS IT?
I DON'T KNOW BUT IT'S COMING FROM THE HOUSE!
COME ON!
Oh... gee!
My alien!
MY NAME IS AELFYRE WHITEMANE THOUGH MY FRIENDS CALL ME WHITEY...
...AND I HOPE TO BE YOUR WORLD'S SALVATION!
THAT RUMBLING FROM THE SNARK CRUISER WOULD HAVE AWAKENED THE DEAD--
--AND I AM NOT DEAD...YET!
COME WITH ME!
13

MEANWHILE...
RRRMMM
JACK, HOW CAN WE SAVE MOM AND DAD? WE CAN'T FIGHT SOMETHING LIKE *THAT!*
OH, LORD, JIM! WHAT IS THAT THING?
WHERE ARE THE CHILDREN?! WHAT'S HAPPENED TO THEM?!
ALEX! JULIE! JACK! KATIE!
MO-- MUMPH!
JACK! *SSSHHH!* THE *MONSTERS!* THEY'VE COME OUT OF THEIR SHIP...
"...AND THEY'RE HEADING TOWARD THE HOUSE! THEY'RE MOVING SO *FAST!*"
MARGARET! GET INSIDE! QUICK!
YAAARGH!
14

JULIE, LET ME GO!
MOM! DAD!
JACK-- DON'T!
DROP THEM, DOG BREATH!
THUD!
LEAVE THEM ALONE!
⟨LIEUTENANT! REMOVE THIS HATCHLING!⟩*
⟨IMMEDIATELY, SIR!⟩
*TRANSLATED FROM THE SNARK
⟨LOOK WHAT ATTACKED ME FROM THE BRUSH!⟩
JULIE-- WHY DIDN'T YOU STAY HIDDEN?
WHY DIDN'T YOU?
⟨THE HUMAN YOUNG HAVE MORE SPIRIT THAN THEIR ELDERS, IT APPEARS...
⟨...BUT WE HAVE NO USE FOR THEM!⟩
⟨KILL THE BOY FIRST!⟩

HOLY COW! THE AIR AROUND ME-- IT'S SHIMMERING! AND I'M NOT FALLING ANYMORE!
< THE BOY IS NOT YOUR ENEMY, MONSTER! >
SKRAK!
WHAT'S GOING ON? WHO ARE YOU?
WHAT ARE THEY?
< I AM! >
MY ENERGY BOLT STUNNED HIM! AND MY GRAVITY FIELD WILL SOON HAVE YOU SAFELY ON THE GROUND!
THEY ARE Z'NRX! AN UNPRONOUNCEABLE NAME! I CALL THEM SNARKS --FROM A POEM BY YOUR LEWIS CARROLL!
BUT WHO--?
LATER! GET BEHIND ME!
< WE WERE TOLD THAT YOUR SMARTSHIP HAD BEEN DESTROYED, KYMELLIAN... AND YOU, WITH IT! >
< IT SEEMS YOU WERE MISINFORMED! >
< NOW, GIVE ME THE GIRL! >

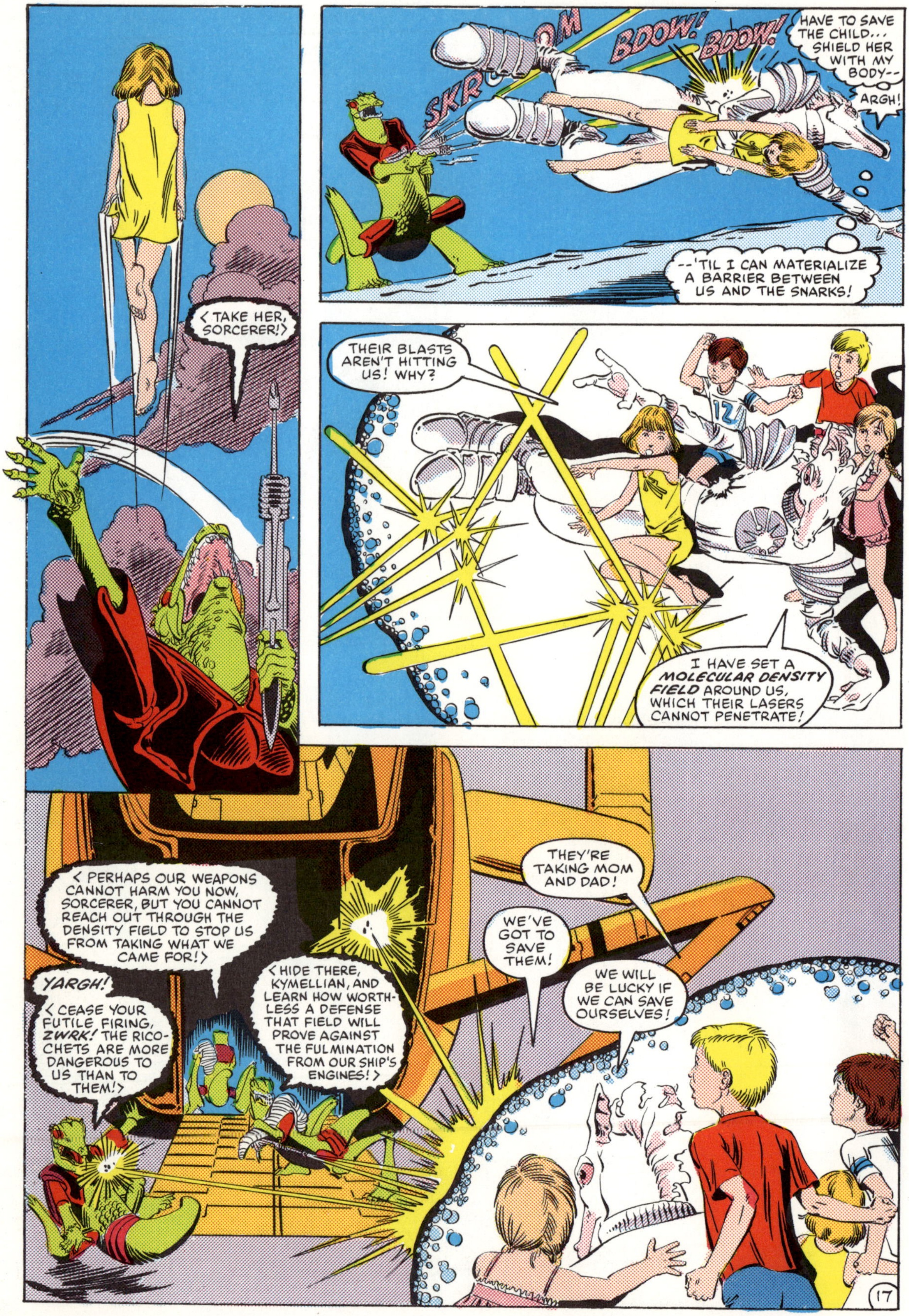
HAVE TO SAVE THE CHILD... SHIELD HER WITH MY BODY--
ARGH!
SKRUMM
BDOW!
BDOW!
--'TIL I CAN MATERIALIZE A BARRIER BETWEEN US AND THE SNARKS!
< TAKE HER, SORCERER! >
THEIR BLASTS AREN'T HITTING US! WHY?
I HAVE SET A ***MOLECULAR DENSITY FIELD*** AROUND US, WHICH THEIR LASERS CANNOT PENETRATE!
< PERHAPS OUR WEAPONS CANNOT HARM YOU NOW, SORCERER, BUT YOU CANNOT REACH OUT THROUGH THE DENSITY FIELD TO STOP US FROM TAKING WHAT WE CAME FOR! >
YARGH!
< CEASE YOUR FUTILE FIRING, ***ZWRK!*** THE RICOCHETS ARE MORE DANGEROUS TO US THAN TO THEM! >
< HIDE THERE, KYMELLIAN, AND LEARN HOW WORTHLESS A DEFENSE THAT FIELD WILL PROVE AGAINST THE FULMINATION FROM OUR SHIP'S ENGINES! >
THEY'RE TAKING MOM AND DAD!
WE'VE GOT TO SAVE THEM!
WE WILL BE LUCKY IF WE CAN SAVE OURSELVES!

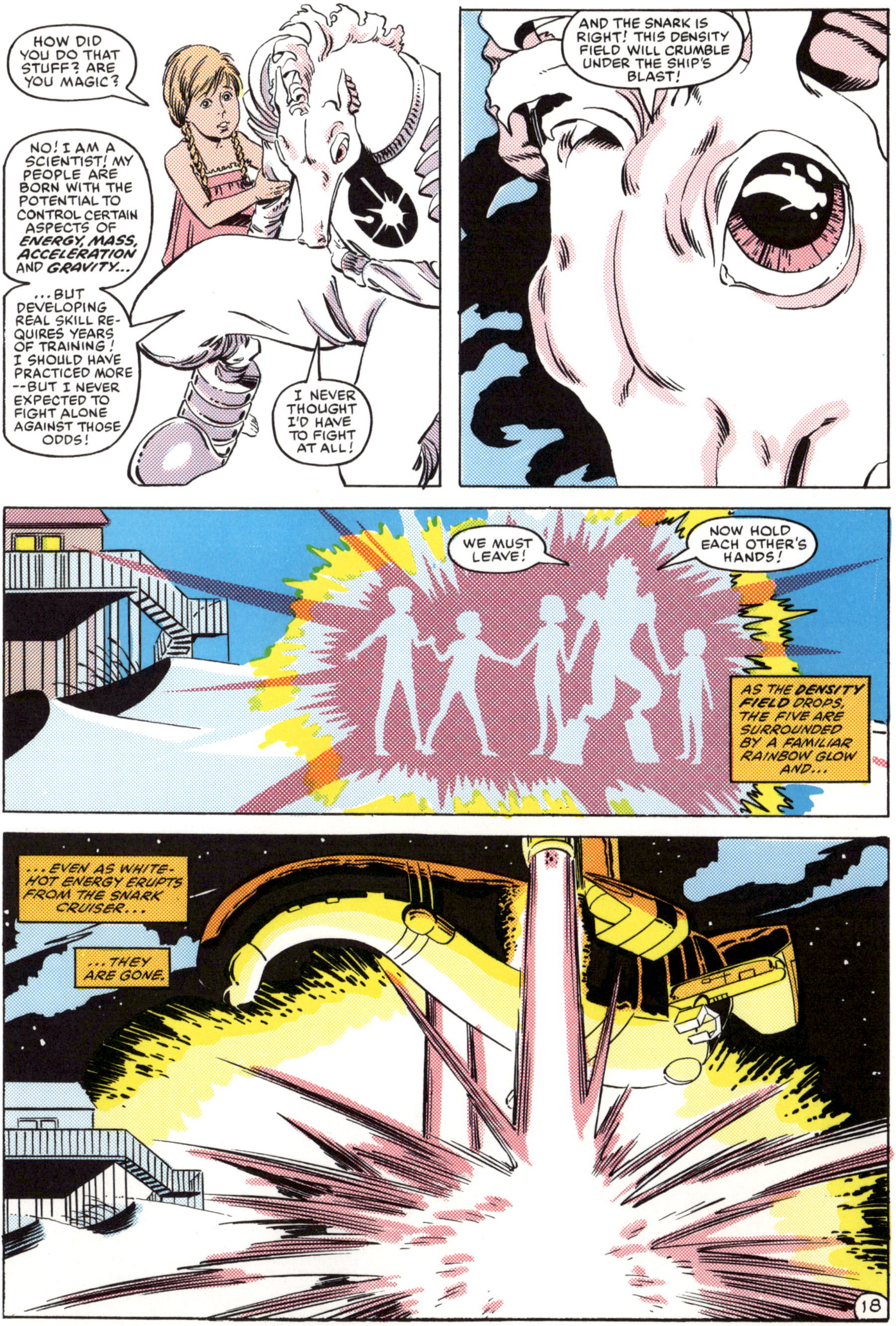

HOW DID YOU DO THAT STUFF? ARE YOU MAGIC?
NO! I AM A SCIENTIST! MY PEOPLE ARE BORN WITH THE POTENTIAL TO CONTROL CERTAIN ASPECTS OF ENERGY, MASS, ACCELERATION AND GRAVITY...
...BUT DEVELOPING REAL SKILL REQUIRES YEARS OF TRAINING! I SHOULD HAVE PRACTICED MORE --BUT I NEVER EXPECTED TO FIGHT ALONE AGAINST THOSE ODDS!
I NEVER THOUGHT I'D HAVE TO FIGHT AT ALL!
AND THE SNARK IS RIGHT! THIS DENSITY FIELD WILL CRUMBLE UNDER THE SHIP'S BLAST!
WE MUST LEAVE!
NOW HOLD EACH OTHER'S HANDS!
AS THE DENSITY FIELD DROPS, THE FIVE ARE SURROUNDED BY A FAMILIAR RAINBOW GLOW AND...
...EVEN AS WHITE-HOT ENERGY ERUPTS FROM THE SNARK CRUISER...
...THEY ARE GONE.

HEY, WE'RE ON THE BEACH!
IT IS A USEFUL WAY TO TRAVEL, BUT IT WORKS ONLY FOR VERY SHORT DISTANCES. MY FATHER... HE CAN ACTUALLY FLY!
YOU WOULD NOT BELIEVE ALL THE WONDERFUL THINGS HE CAN D--UGH!
YOU'RE HURT, WHITEY.
BADLY, I FEAR! AND THE EFFORT OF TRANSPORTING US HERE HAS SAPPED MUCH OF MY STRENGTH!
WE MUST LEAVE! THE SNARKS ASSUME WE HAVE BEEN DESTROYED, BUT THEY WILL SOON REALIZE THEIR MISTAKE. AND WHEN THEY DO, THEY WILL COME FOR US!
FRIDAY, CAN YOU TAKE US AWAY FROM HERE?
I HAVE LOST WARP-DRIVE, RADAR AND MOST COMMUNICATIONS FUNCTIONS BUT MY GRAVITY/ANTI-GRAVITY PODS ARE INTACT.
I CAN STILL FLY, BUT I CANNOT GO FAR--OR FAST!
THE COST OF THIS VENTURE IS HIGH! FIRST THESE CHILDREN'S PARENTS--THEN YOU, FRIDAY!
YOU ARE NOT IN GREAT SHAPE, YOURSELF!
I HAVE BEEN TAUGHT NOT TO KILL... BUT I WISH I HAD KILLED THEM, ANYWAY! I NEVER REALIZED THAT THE SNARKS WERE SO EVIL... AND DEADLY!
THEY HAVE WHAT THEY WANT NOW, AND I FEAR IT IS MY FAULT!

THEY WANTED OUR PARENTS?
WHY?
IT IS A LONG STORY.
MY SCIENCE IS THE STUDY OF ALIEN RACES AND YOU HUMANS WERE MY FIRST ASSIGNMENT. IN MONITORING EARTH'S COMPUTERS...
"...I LEARNED THAT YOUR FATHER HAD DISCOVERED THE MATTER/ANTI-MATTER CONVERSION THAT IS MY PEOPLES' MAIN SOURCE OF ENERGY.
"IT IS ONE OF THE MOST CLOSELY GUARDED SECRETS IN THE GALAXY... AND FOR GOOD REASON.
"THE FIRST TESTING OF THE FORMULA TOTALLY DESTROYED OUR PLANET, AND HAD WE NOT, BY THAT TIME, BEEN A SPACE-FARING RACE, NONE OF US WOULD HAVE SURVIVED!
"I SENT A MESSAGE TO MY PEOPLE TELLING THEM OF YOUR FATHER'S DISCOVERY AND ASKING PERMISSION TO WARN HIM, DESPITE OUR LAWS THAT FORBID INTERFERENCE.
"THE SNARKS INTERCEPTED MY TRANSMISSION, JAMMED IT, AND BLEW *FRIDAY* FROM THE SKY.
"THEN THEY KIDNAPPED YOUR FATHER. THEY PLAN TO USE HIS FORMULA AS A WEAPON TO CONQUER THEIR GALAXY!"
BUT IF YOU'RE NOT SUPPOSED TO INTERFERE, WHY DID YOU TRY TO SAVE THE EARTH TO BEGIN WITH?
I CAME TO LOVE YOUR WRITINGS! THE BEAUTY AND VARIETY OF HUMAN LITERATURE IS BEYOND PRICE AND IT WOULD BE TRAGIC WERE SUCH A TREASURE TO BE LOST TO OUR GALAXY!
MAYBE FRIDAY WAS RIGHT. PERHAPS WE SHOULD LET THE SNARKS TEST YOUR FATHER'S FORMULA. LET THEM DESTROY THEIR *OWN* UGLY WORLD AND LEAVE YOUR EARTH IN PEACE!
BUT...DAD'S *LAB* IS GOING TO TEST HIS FORMULA... *TOMORROW!* DAD INVENTED A MACHINE TO DO IT! I'VE SEEN THE BLUEPRINTS, THEY'RE UP AT THE HOUSE.
MAYBE I SHOULD GO GET THEM, IN CASE THE SNARKS COME BACK!

"IT'LL ONLY TAKE A MINUTE!"
WHITEY, I'VE GOT 'EM!
GOOD! NOW LET US LEAVE!
SOON...
YOUR FATHER MUST BE A GREAT GENIUS TO HAVE WORKED OUT THIS EQUATION UNDER YOUR WORLD'S PRIMITIVE CONDITIONS.
IT APPEARS THAT, TOMORROW, HIS TEST WILL BE FAR MORE SUCCESSFUL THAN HE PLANNED. YOUR TECHNOLOGY CANNOT PREVENT IT FROM DESTROYING YOUR PLANET...
...AND I AM NOT ALLOWED TO INTERFERE!
YOU'VE GOT TO DO SOMETHING!
WITHOUT PERMISSION I CAN PERHAPS SAVE YOU, BUT YOUR WORLD... YOUR CIVILIZATION...IS SURELY DOOMED.
FRIDAY, PROVIDE THESE CHILDREN WITH PLACES TO SLEEP...
...WHILE I THINK WHAT CAN BE DONE!
FRIDAY'S WALLS SHIFT AND REFORM TO COMPLY WITH WHITEY'S REQUEST.
I'M SCARED! BUT I'VE GOT TO BE BRAVE! I'M A BIG GIRL NOW! I WON'T CRY! I WON'T!
ALEX... I WANT TO GO HOME!
I KNOW, BABY!
THIS IS STUPID! I WISH KATE'D NEVER SEEN THIS DUMB SHIP!

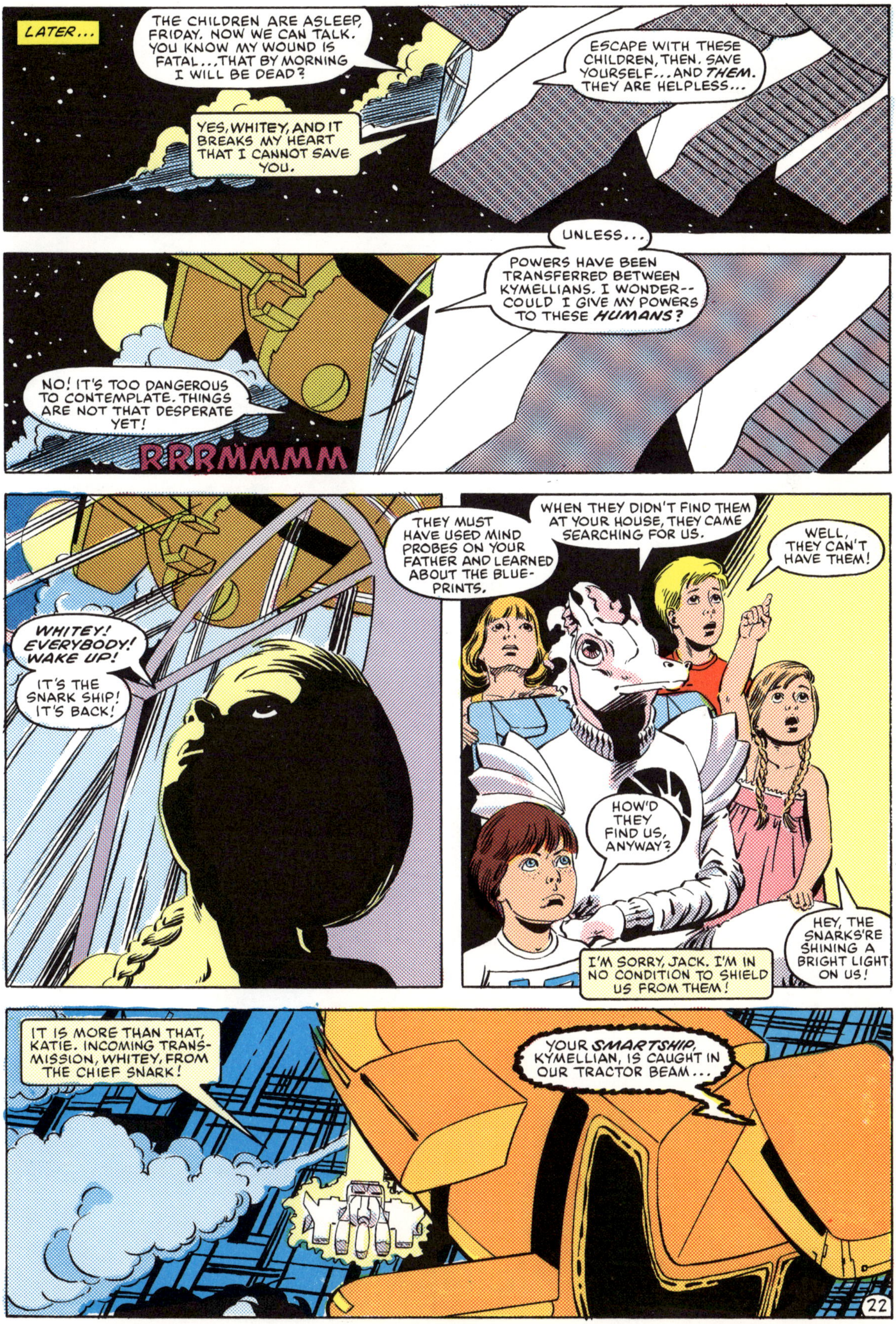

LATER...
THE CHILDREN ARE ASLEEP, FRIDAY. NOW WE CAN TALK. YOU KNOW MY WOUND IS FATAL...THAT BY MORNING I WILL BE DEAD?
YES, WHITEY, AND IT BREAKS MY HEART THAT I CANNOT SAVE YOU.
ESCAPE WITH THESE CHILDREN, THEN. SAVE YOURSELF...AND THEM. THEY ARE HELPLESS...
UNLESS...
POWERS HAVE BEEN TRANSFERRED BETWEEN KYMELLIANS. I WONDER-- COULD I GIVE MY POWERS TO THESE HUMANS?
NO! IT'S TOO DANGEROUS TO CONTEMPLATE. THINGS ARE NOT THAT DESPERATE YET!
RRRMMMM
WHITEY! EVERYBODY! WAKE UP!
IT'S THE SNARK SHIP! IT'S BACK!
THEY MUST HAVE USED MIND PROBES ON YOUR FATHER AND LEARNED ABOUT THE BLUE-PRINTS.
WHEN THEY DIDN'T FIND THEM AT YOUR HOUSE, THEY CAME SEARCHING FOR US.
WELL, THEY CAN'T HAVE THEM!
HOW'D THEY FIND US, ANYWAY?
HEY, THE SNARKS'RE SHINING A BRIGHT LIGHT ON US!
I'M SORRY, JACK. I'M IN NO CONDITION TO SHIELD US FROM THEM!
IT IS MORE THAN THAT, KATIE. INCOMING TRANS-MISSION, WHITEY, FROM THE CHIEF SNARK!
YOUR SMARTSHIP, KYMELLIAN, IS CAUGHT IN OUR TRACTOR BEAM...

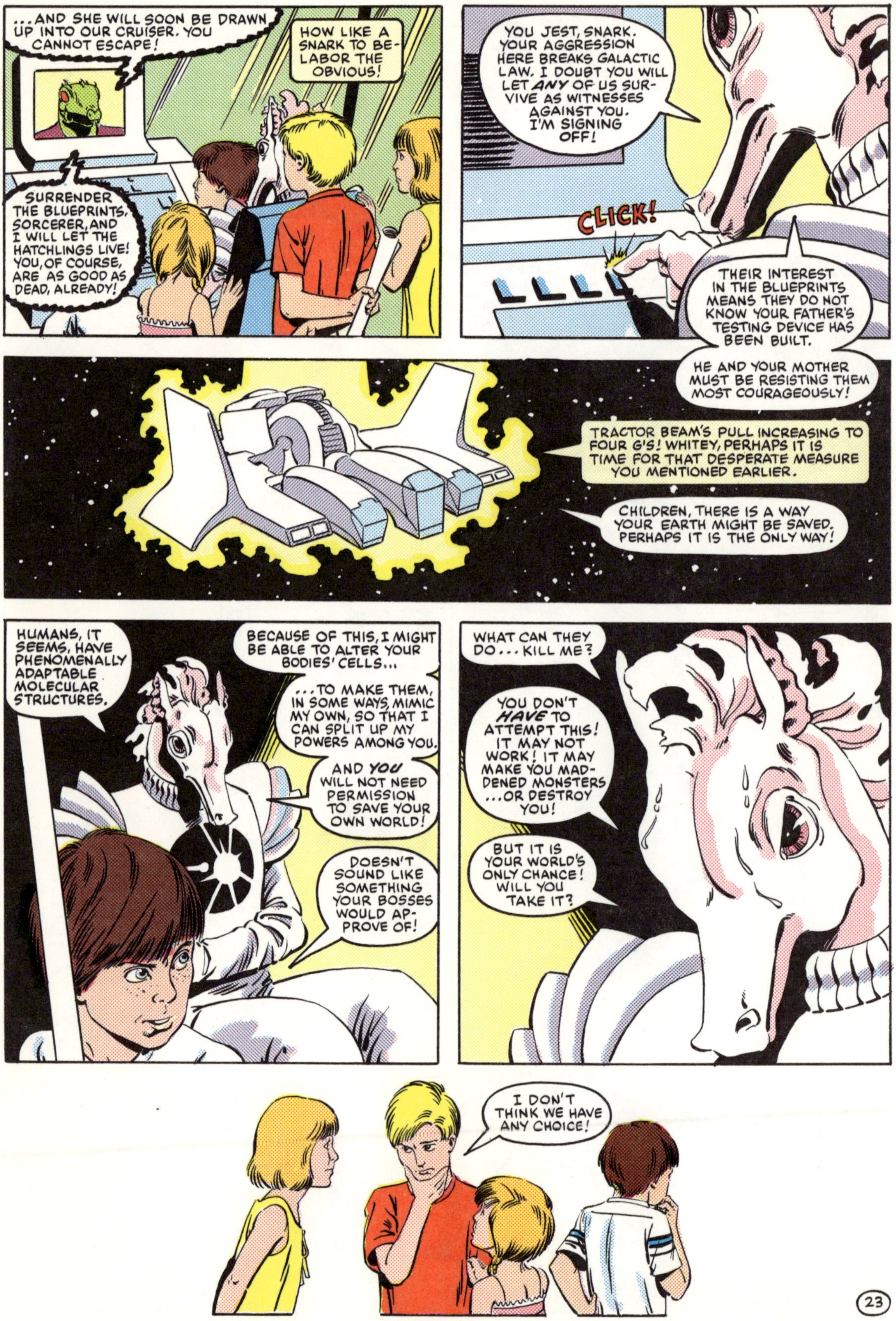
...AND SHE WILL SOON BE DRAWN UP INTO OUR CRUISER. YOU CANNOT ESCAPE!
HOW LIKE A SNARK TO BELABOR THE OBVIOUS!
SURRENDER THE BLUEPRINTS, SORCERER, AND I WILL LET THE HATCHLINGS LIVE! YOU, OF COURSE, ARE AS GOOD AS DEAD, ALREADY!
YOU JEST, SNARK. YOUR AGGRESSION HERE BREAKS GALACTIC LAW. I DOUBT YOU WILL LET ANY OF US SURVIVE AS WITNESSES AGAINST YOU. I'M SIGNING OFF!
CLICK!
THEIR INTEREST IN THE BLUEPRINTS MEANS THEY DO NOT KNOW YOUR FATHER'S TESTING DEVICE HAS BEEN BUILT.
HE AND YOUR MOTHER MUST BE RESISTING THEM MOST COURAGEOUSLY!
TRACTOR BEAM'S PULL INCREASING TO FOUR G'S! WHITEY, PERHAPS IT IS TIME FOR THAT DESPERATE MEASURE YOU MENTIONED EARLIER.
CHILDREN, THERE IS A WAY YOUR EARTH MIGHT BE SAVED. PERHAPS IT IS THE ONLY WAY!
HUMANS, IT SEEMS, HAVE PHENOMENALLY ADAPTABLE MOLECULAR STRUCTURES.
BECAUSE OF THIS, I MIGHT BE ABLE TO ALTER YOUR BODIES' CELLS...
...TO MAKE THEM, IN SOME WAYS, MIMIC MY OWN, SO THAT I CAN SPLIT UP MY POWERS AMONG YOU.
AND YOU WILL NOT NEED PERMISSION TO SAVE YOUR OWN WORLD!
DOESN'T SOUND LIKE SOMETHING YOUR BOSSES WOULD APPROVE OF!
WHAT CAN THEY DO... KILL ME?
YOU DON'T HAVE TO ATTEMPT THIS! IT MAY NOT WORK! IT MAY MAKE YOU MADDENED MONSTERS ...OR DESTROY YOU!
BUT IT IS YOUR WORLD'S ONLY CHANCE! WILL YOU TAKE IT?
I DON'T THINK WE HAVE ANY CHOICE!

HURRY, WHITEY, THEY'RE INCREASING THE PULL TO FIVE G'S!
THEN WE HAVEN'T A SECOND TO LOSE. KNEEL BESIDE ME--QUICKLY--AND TAKE MY HANDS!
MAYBE NOT, JACK, BUT AT LEAST WE CAN TRY!
This is stupid! It isn't going to work!
A BLINDING FLASH OF ENERGY SURROUNDS THE CHILDREN, JOLTS THROUGH THEM LIKE AN ELECTRICAL CURRENT...
SAVE YOUR ...WORLD...
THEN SUDDENLY IT IS OVER.
HE'S DISAPPEARING ...IN A BUNCH OF SPARKLES, LIKE FAIRY DUST!
YEAH, AND THAT FLASHING LIGHT DIDN'T LAST LONG ENOUGH TO DO ANYTHING! I'D SAY WE'VE BEEN HAD!
MY ALIEN!
FRIDAY, HE DIDN'T TELL US HE WOULD DIE!
24

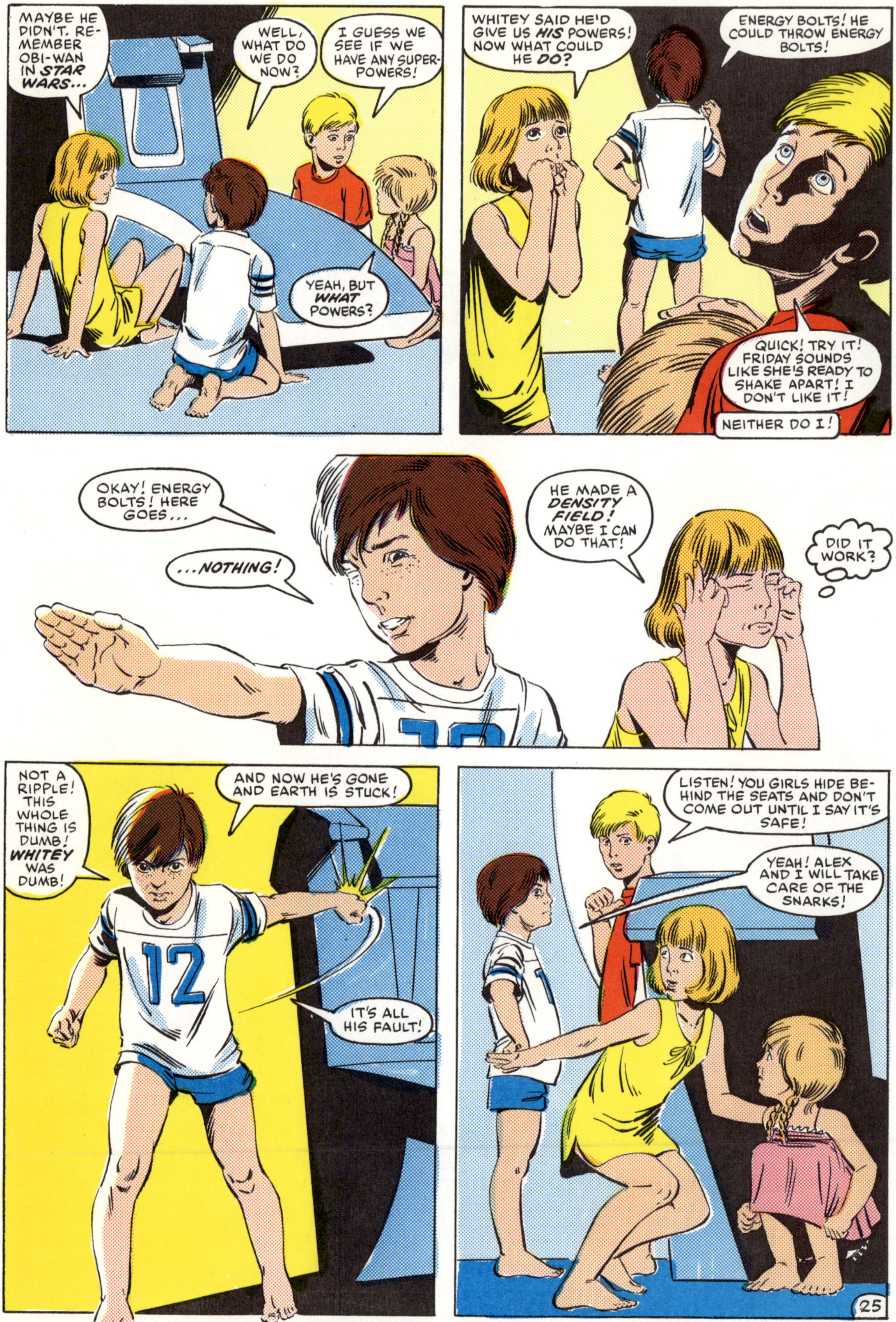
MAYBE HE DIDN'T RE-MEMBER OBI-WAN IN STAR WARS...
WELL, WHAT DO WE DO NOW?
I GUESS WE SEE IF WE HAVE ANY SUPER-POWERS!
YEAH, BUT WHAT POWERS?
WHITEY SAID HE'D GIVE US HIS POWERS! NOW WHAT COULD HE DO?
ENERGY BOLTS! HE COULD THROW ENERGY BOLTS!
QUICK! TRY IT! FRIDAY SOUNDS LIKE SHE'S READY TO SHAKE APART! I DON'T LIKE IT!
NEITHER DO I!
OKAY! ENERGY BOLTS! HERE GOES...
...NOTHING!
HE MADE A DENSITY FIELD! MAYBE I CAN DO THAT!
DID IT WORK?
NOT A RIPPLE! THIS WHOLE THING IS DUMB! WHITEY WAS DUMB!
AND NOW HE'S GONE AND EARTH IS STUCK!
IT'S ALL HIS FAULT!
LISTEN! YOU GIRLS HIDE BE-HIND THE SEATS AND DON'T COME OUT UNTIL I SAY IT'S SAFE!
YEAH! ALEX AND I WILL TAKE CARE OF THE SNARKS!
12
25

HEY, WAIT A MINUTE! "HIDE BEHIND THE SEATS?"
GIVE ME A BREAK!
MALE CHAUVINIST PIGS!
OINK! OINK!!!
JUST BECAUSE WE'RE SCARED...
...DOESN'T MEAN THAT WE CAN'T FIGHT TOO!
ALL RIIIIGHT!
Not bad, huh, Jack!
Yeah, for a couple of girls, they're okay!
ALL RIGHT, THEN! WHEN THEY COME FOR US, WE'LL BE READY...
...THE FOUR OF US TOGETHER!
NO MATTER HOW STUPID IT ALL SEEMS!

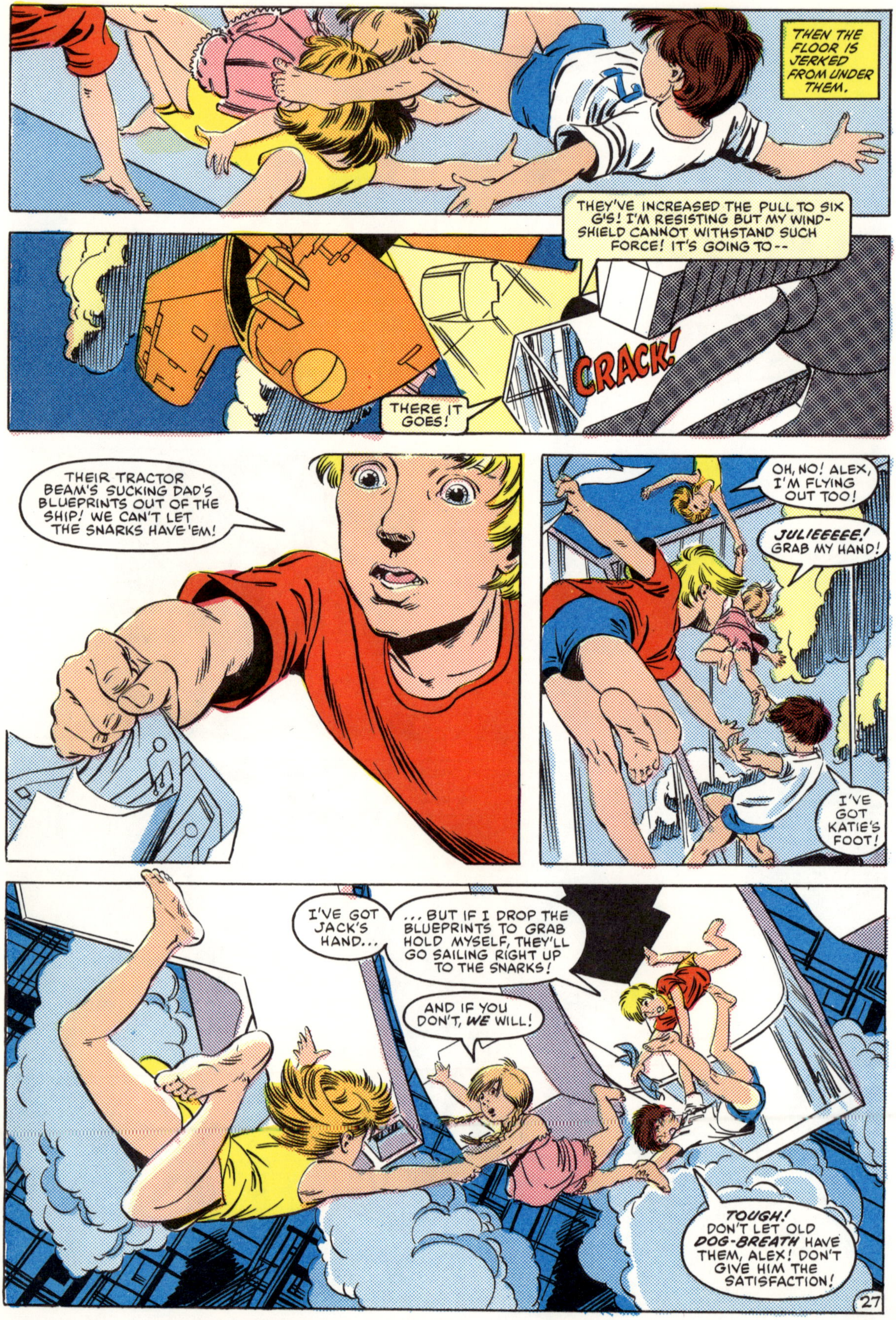
THEN THE FLOOR IS JERKED FROM UNDER THEM.
THEY'VE INCREASED THE PULL TO SIX G'S! I'M RESISTING BUT MY WIND-SHIELD CANNOT WITHSTAND SUCH FORCE! IT'S GOING TO--
CRACK!
THERE IT GOES!
THEIR TRACTOR BEAM'S SUCKING DAD'S BLUEPRINTS OUT OF THE SHIP! WE CAN'T LET THE SNARKS HAVE 'EM!
OH, NO! ALEX, I'M FLYING OUT TOO!
JULIEEEEE! GRAB MY HAND!
I'VE GOT KATIE'S FOOT!
I'VE GOT JACK'S HAND...
... BUT IF I DROP THE BLUEPRINTS TO GRAB HOLD MYSELF, THEY'LL GO SAILING RIGHT UP TO THE SNARKS!
AND IF YOU DON'T, WE WILL!
TOUGH! DON'T LET OLD DOG-BREATH HAVE THEM, ALEX! DON'T GIVE HIM THE SATISFACTION!

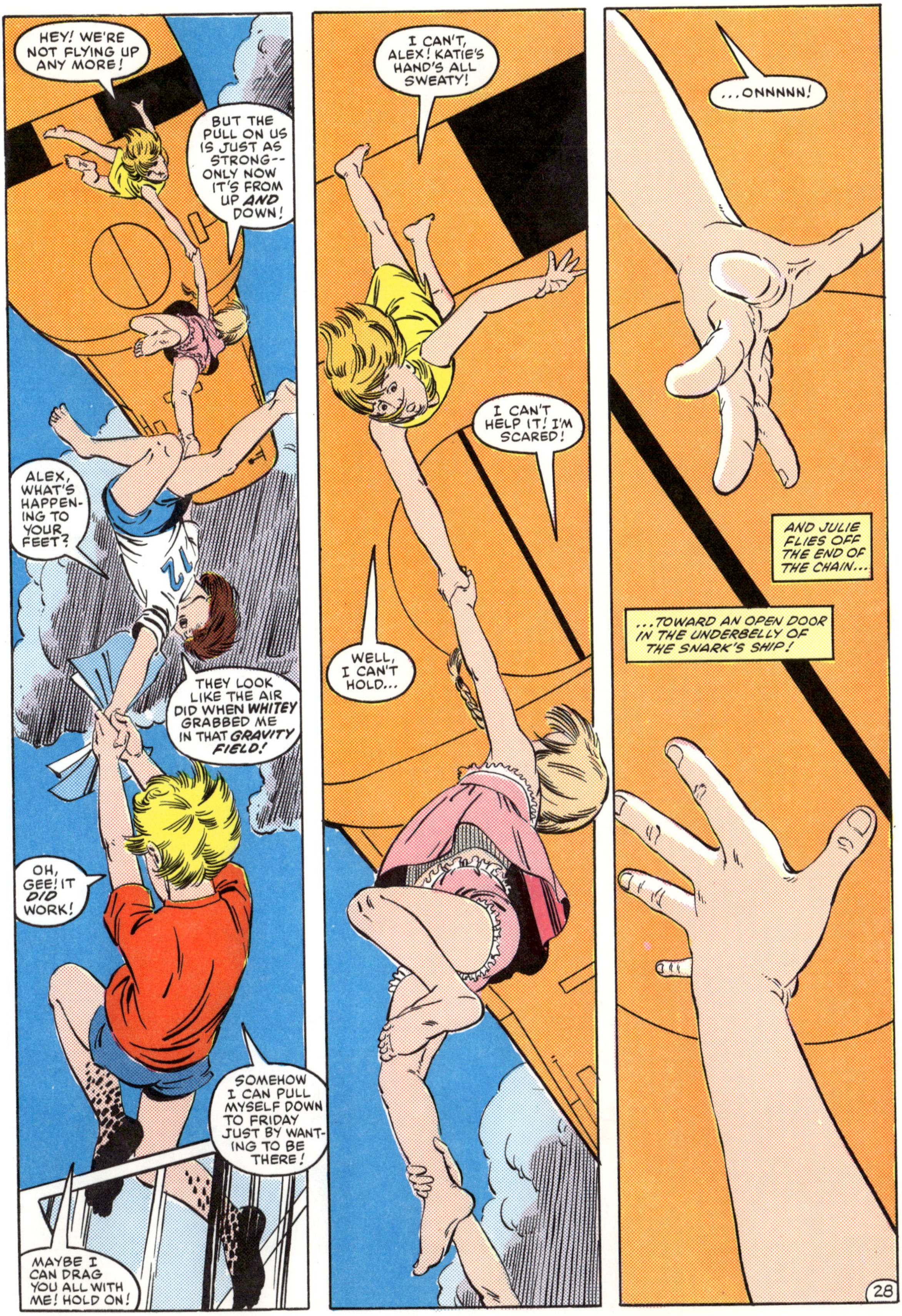
HEY! WE'RE NOT FLYING UP ANY MORE!
BUT THE PULL ON US IS JUST AS STRONG-- ONLY NOW IT'S FROM UP AND DOWN!
ALEX, WHAT'S HAPPEN-ING TO YOUR FEET?
THEY LOOK LIKE THE AIR DID WHEN WHITEY GRABBED ME IN THAT GRAVITY FIELD!
OH, GEE! IT DID WORK!
SOMEHOW I CAN PULL MYSELF DOWN TO FRIDAY JUST BY WANT-ING TO BE THERE!
MAYBE I CAN DRAG YOU ALL WITH ME! HOLD ON!
I CAN'T, ALEX! KATIE'S HAND'S ALL SWEATY!
I CAN'T HELP IT! I'M SCARED!
WELL, I CAN'T HOLD...
...ONNNNN!
AND JULIE FLIES OFF THE END OF THE CHAIN...
...TOWARD AN OPEN DOOR IN THE UNDERBELLY OF THE SNARK'S SHIP!

AND INSIDE...
<GOT HER!>
<THE HATCHLING DOESN'T LOOK SO COURAGEOUS NOW!>
NO! KEEP AWAY FROM--
...MEEEEEEEE!
AND IN A FLASH OF LIGHT AND COLOR SHE IS GONE, TRAILING A RAINBOW BEHIND HER!
<THE HATCHLING CAN FLY...SO FAST WE CAN HARDLY SEE HER! SHE APPEARS AS SURPRISED AS WE ARE!>
<THE SORCERER MUST HAVE DIED AND GIVEN HIS POWERS ONTO THESE HUMANS!>
<A KYMELLIAN CAN TRANSFER POWER TO SOMEONE OF ANOTHER WORLD? THE QUEEN MOTHER WILL REWARD US FOR THIS INFORMATION...>
<...AS SHE WILL FOR THE CAPTURE OF THESE HATCHLINGS. ONCE TAMED, THEIR KYMELLIAN POWERS WILL MAKE THEM IMPRESSIVE WEAPONS IN HER ARSENAL!>
<SEIZE THE GIRL-CHILD AND BRING HER TO ME! I WILL SEE TO THE CAPTURE OF THE OTHERS!>
WHILE OUTSIDE...
KATIE, YOUR ANKLE! IT-- IT'S--
YOOWW!
ALEX, HER ANKLE-- IT BURNED MY HAND! I COULDN'T HOLD ON!

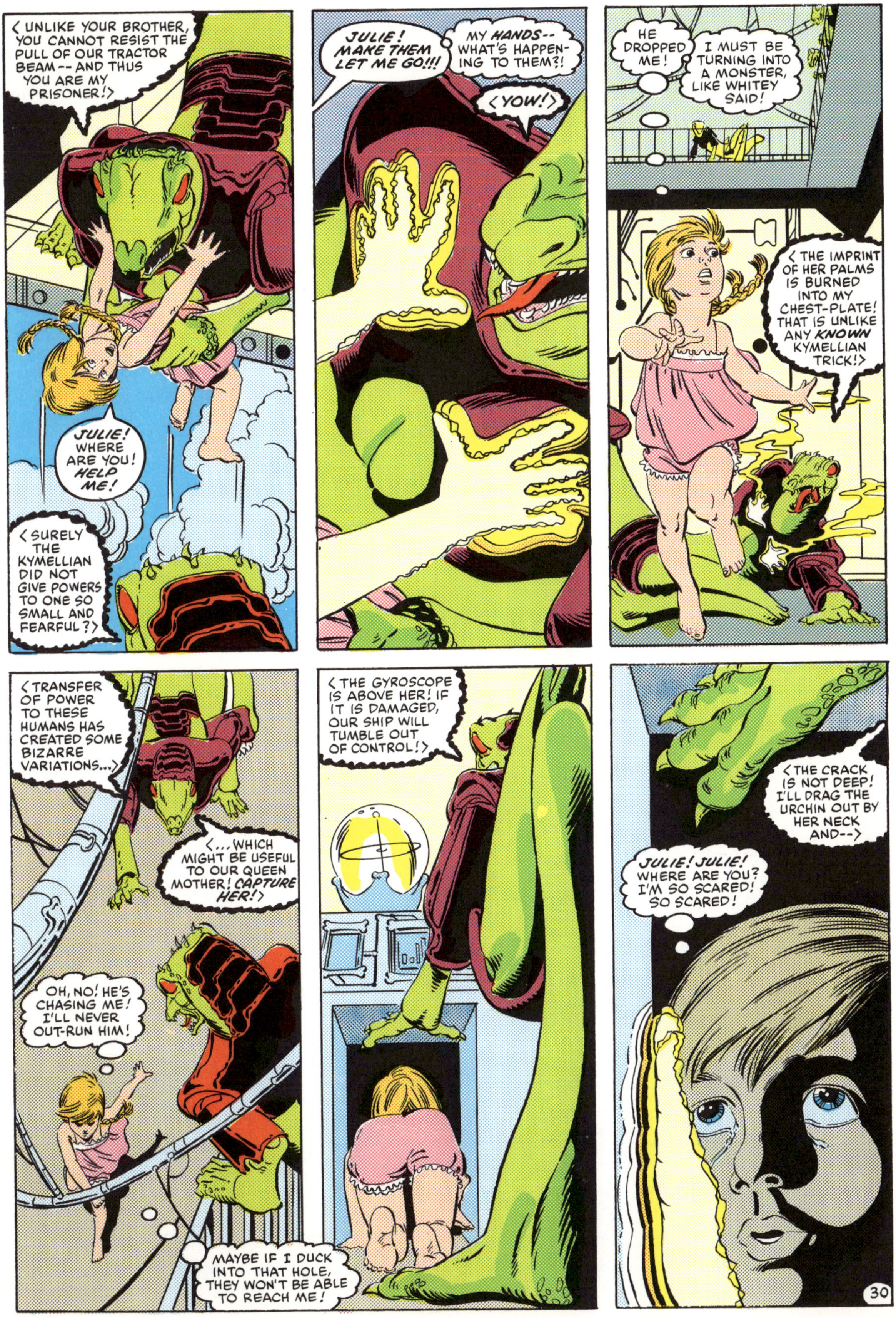
< UNLIKE YOUR BROTHER, YOU CANNOT RESIST THE PULL OF OUR TRACTOR BEAM -- AND THUS YOU ARE MY PRISONER!>
JULIE! WHERE ARE YOU! HELP ME!
< SURELY THE KYMELLIAN DID NOT GIVE POWERS TO ONE SO SMALL AND FEARFUL?>
JULIE! MAKE THEM LET ME GO!!!
MY HANDS-- WHAT'S HAPPENING TO THEM?!
< YOW!>
HE DROPPED ME!
I MUST BE TURNING INTO A MONSTER, LIKE WHITEY SAID!
< THE IMPRINT OF HER PALMS IS BURNED INTO MY CHEST-PLATE! THAT IS UNLIKE ANY KNOWN KYMELLIAN TRICK!>
< TRANSFER OF POWER TO THESE HUMANS HAS CREATED SOME BIZARRE VARIATIONS...>
<... WHICH MIGHT BE USEFUL TO OUR QUEEN MOTHER! CAPTURE HER!>
OH, NO! HE'S CHASING ME! I'LL NEVER OUT-RUN HIM!
MAYBE IF I DUCK INTO THAT HOLE, THEY WON'T BE ABLE TO REACH ME!
< THE GYROSCOPE IS ABOVE HER! IF IT IS DAMAGED, OUR SHIP WILL TUMBLE OUT OF CONTROL!>
< THE CRACK IS NOT DEEP! I'LL DRAG THE URCHIN OUT BY HER NECK AND-->
JULIE! JULIE! WHERE ARE YOU? I'M SO SCARED! SO SCARED!

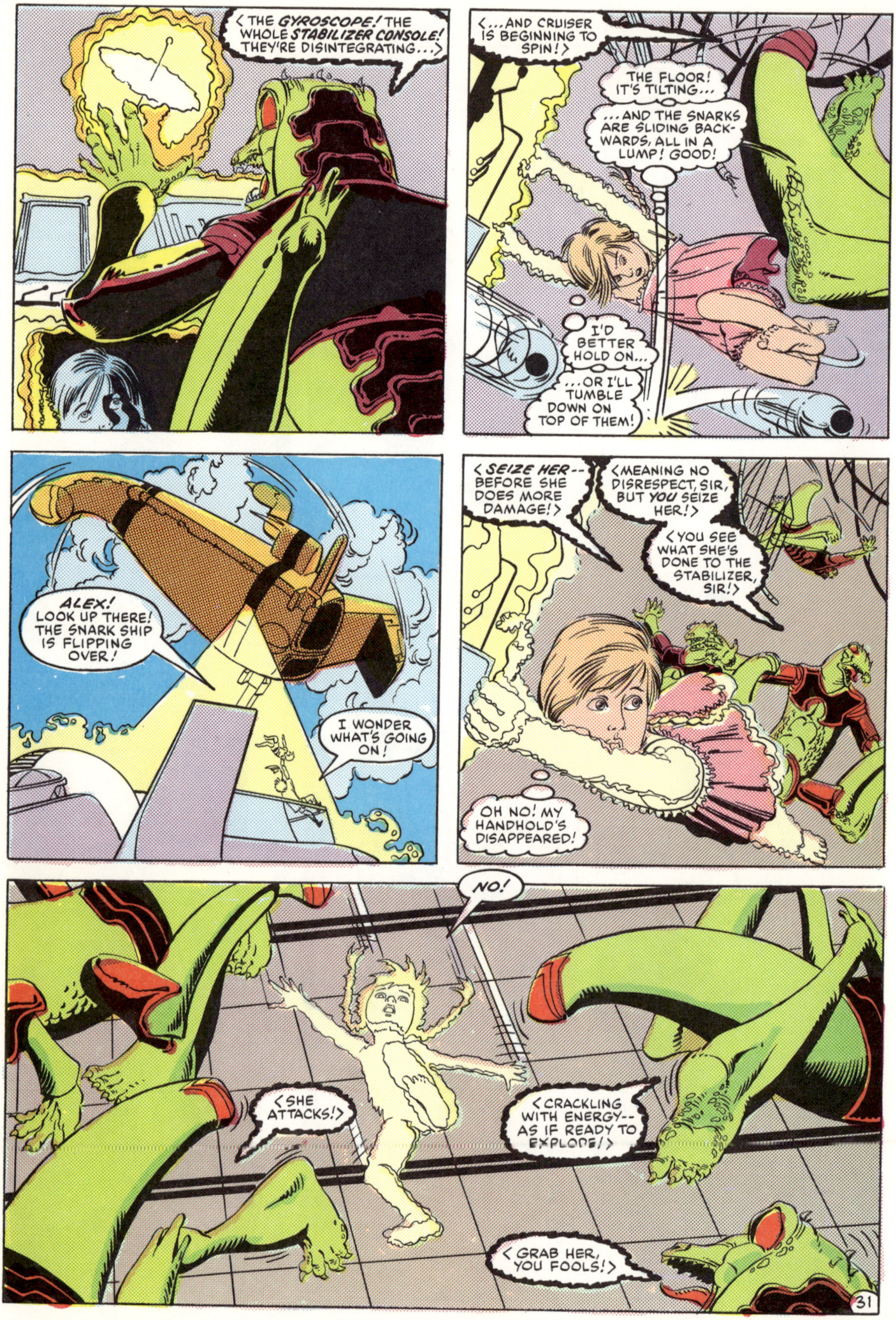
<THE GYROSCOPE! THE WHOLE STABILIZER CONSOLE! THEY'RE DISINTEGRATING...>
<...AND CRUISER IS BEGINNING TO SPIN!>
THE FLOOR! IT'S TILTING...
...AND THE SNARKS ARE SLIDING BACKWARDS, ALL IN A LUMP! GOOD!
I'D BETTER HOLD ON...
...OR I'LL TUMBLE DOWN ON TOP OF THEM!
ALEX! LOOK UP THERE! THE SNARK SHIP IS FLIPPING OVER!
I WONDER WHAT'S GOING ON!
<SEIZE HER-- BEFORE SHE DOES MORE DAMAGE!>
<MEANING NO DISRESPECT, SIR, BUT YOU SEIZE HER!>
<YOU SEE WHAT SHE'S DONE TO THE STABILIZER, SIR!>
OH NO! MY HANDHOLD'S DISAPPEARED!
NO!
<SHE ATTACKS!>
<CRACKLING WITH ENERGY-- AS IF READY TO EXPLODE!>
<GRAB HER, YOU FOOLS!>

< SHE'S SLIDING TOWARD THE TRACTOR BEAM CONTROLS! >
CRASH!
AND OUTSIDE...
HOLY COW! NOW THE TRACTOR BEAM'S SHUT OFF!
WATCH IT, JACK! YOU'RE FALLING ON TOP OF ME!
THAT COULDN'T BE KATIE'S DOING--COULD IT?! SHE'S ALWAYS BREAKING THINGS...
BUT HOW COULD A LITTLE GIRL BREAK AN ENTIRE STARSHIP?
OH WOW! ENERGY BALLS! LIKE WHITEY'S!
...ONLY I HAVE TO POWER UP--DISINTEGRATE STUFF BEFORE I CAN SHOOT THEM OFF! AND THEN THEY GO EVERYWHERE!
I'LL HAVE TO PRACTICE, LIKE HE SAID, TO GET GOOD AT IT! I CAN'T WAIT TO SHOW THE OTHERS!
BOOM!
DUCK!
BA-BLAM!
KYMELLIAN ENERGY BOLTS!
SHE JUST RIPPED A HOLE IN OUR HULL!
THE SHIP'S ROLLING--AND I'M SLIDING...
...INTO THE HOLE I MADE WITH MY BLAST!
ALEX! SAVE ME!
IT'S KATIE! SHE'S FALLING! JACK, HELP ME UP!
I'VE GOT TO CATCH HER!

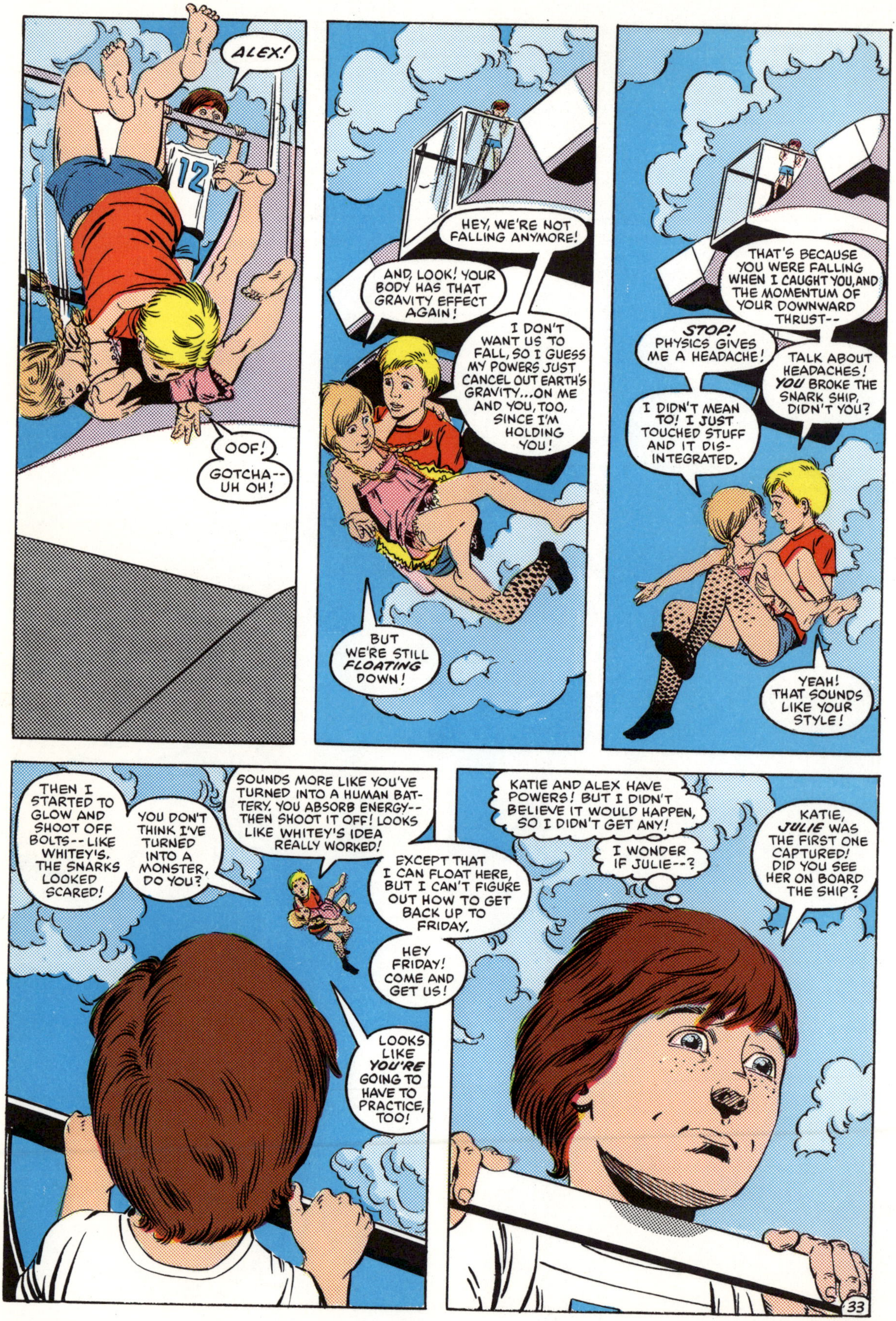
ALEX!
OOF!
GOTCHA--
UH OH!
HEY, WE'RE NOT FALLING ANYMORE!
AND, LOOK! YOUR BODY HAS THAT GRAVITY EFFECT AGAIN!
I DON'T WANT US TO FALL, SO I GUESS MY POWERS JUST CANCEL OUT EARTH'S GRAVITY...ON ME AND YOU, TOO, SINCE I'M HOLDING YOU!
BUT WE'RE STILL FLOATING DOWN!
THAT'S BECAUSE YOU WERE FALLING WHEN I CAUGHT YOU, AND THE MOMENTUM OF YOUR DOWNWARD THRUST--
STOP! PHYSICS GIVES ME A HEADACHE!
TALK ABOUT HEADACHES! YOU BROKE THE SNARK SHIP, DIDN'T YOU?
I DIDN'T MEAN TO! I JUST TOUCHED STUFF AND IT DIS-INTEGRATED.
YEAH! THAT SOUNDS LIKE YOUR STYLE!
THEN I STARTED TO GLOW AND SHOOT OFF BOLTS--LIKE WHITEY'S. THE SNARKS LOOKED SCARED!
YOU DON'T THINK I'VE TURNED INTO A MONSTER, DO YOU?
SOUNDS MORE LIKE YOU'VE TURNED INTO A HUMAN BAT-TERY. YOU ABSORB ENERGY--THEN SHOOT IT OFF! LOOKS LIKE WHITEY'S IDEA REALLY WORKED!
EXCEPT THAT I CAN FLOAT HERE, BUT I CAN'T FIGURE OUT HOW TO GET BACK UP TO FRIDAY.
HEY FRIDAY! COME AND GET US!
LOOKS LIKE YOU'RE GOING TO HAVE TO PRACTICE, TOO!
KATIE AND ALEX HAVE POWERS! BUT I DIDN'T BELIEVE IT WOULD HAPPEN, SO I DIDN'T GET ANY!
I WONDER IF JULIE--?
KATIE, JULIE WAS THE FIRST ONE CAPTURED! DID YOU SEE HER ON BOARD THE SHIP?

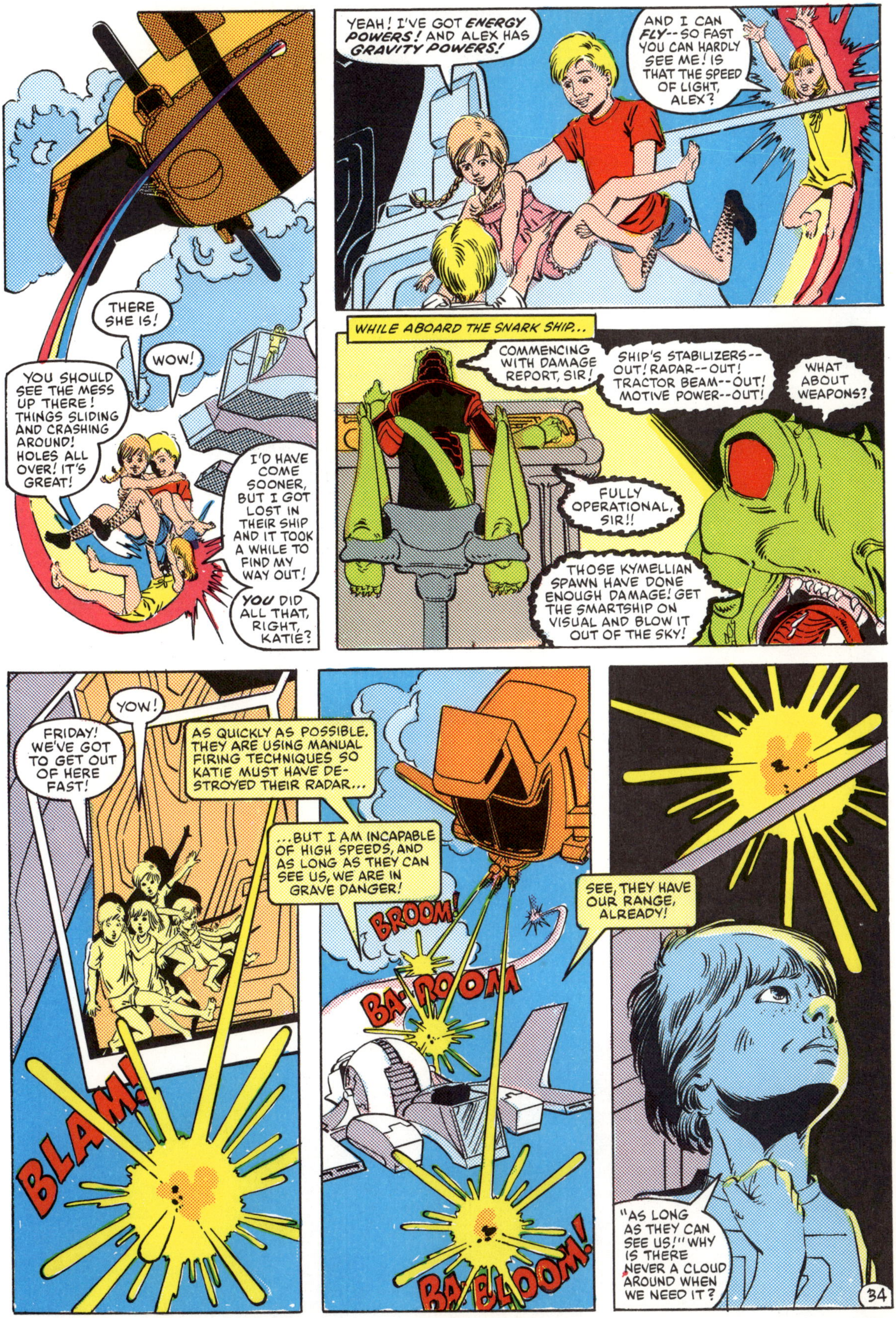

THERE SHE IS!
WOW!
YOU SHOULD SEE THE MESS UP THERE! THINGS SLIDING AND CRASHING AROUND! HOLES ALL OVER! IT'S GREAT!
I'D HAVE COME SOONER, BUT I GOT LOST IN THEIR SHIP AND IT TOOK A WHILE TO FIND MY WAY OUT!
YOU DID ALL THAT, RIGHT, KATIE?
YEAH! I'VE GOT ENERGY POWERS! AND ALEX HAS GRAVITY POWERS!
AND I CAN FLY--SO FAST YOU CAN HARDLY SEE ME! IS THAT THE SPEED OF LIGHT, ALEX?
WHILE ABOARD THE SNARK SHIP...
COMMENCING WITH DAMAGE REPORT, SIR!
SHIP'S STABILIZERS--OUT! RADAR--OUT! TRACTOR BEAM--OUT! MOTIVE POWER--OUT!
WHAT ABOUT WEAPONS?
FULLY OPERATIONAL, SIR!!
THOSE KYMELLIAN SPAWN HAVE DONE ENOUGH DAMAGE! GET THE SMARTSHIP ON VISUAL AND BLOW IT OUT OF THE SKY!
FRIDAY! WE'VE GOT TO GET OUT OF HERE FAST!
YOW!
AS QUICKLY AS POSSIBLE. THEY ARE USING MANUAL FIRING TECHNIQUES SO KATIE MUST HAVE DESTROYED THEIR RADAR...
...BUT I AM INCAPABLE OF HIGH SPEEDS, AND AS LONG AS THEY CAN SEE US, WE ARE IN GRAVE DANGER!
BLAM!
BROOM!
BA-ROOM
BA-BLOOM!
SEE, THEY HAVE OUR RANGE, ALREADY!
"AS LONG AS THEY CAN SEE US!" WHY IS THERE NEVER A CLOUD AROUND WHEN WE NEED IT?

SUDDENLY...
ALEX, WHERE'D THIS FOG COME FROM?
I CAN HARDLY SEE YOU AND KATIE!
AND LOOK! THE SNARKS CAN'T SEE US EITHER! THEIR SHOTS ARE MISSING BY A MILE!
GOSH, JACK! MAYBE YOU HAVE *WISHING* POWERS!
JACK? *JACK!* WHERE ARE YOU?
THERE HE IS!
WE'RE *INSIDE* OF HIM!
HE TURNED INTO A CLOUD!
HOW'D HE DO THAT, ALEX?
WHITEY HAD POWERS OVER *MASS*, TOO. I GUESS JACK CAN CONTROL HIS MASS... HE CAN BECOME A CLOUD WHENEVER HE WANTS TO.
HEY, JACK! ISN'T THIS NEAT?
YEAH! I JUST WISH MY CLOTHES WENT CLOUDY TOO!
FOLLOW FRIDAY AND KEEP BLOCKING HER FROM THE SNARKS!
I'LL GET YOUR CLOTHES FOR YOU!
AND JACK FOLLOWS, A GIANT CLOUD-BOY, TAKING SEVEN-LEAGUE STRIDES OVER A MOONLIT LAND-SCAPE...
...LEAVING THE SNARK'S SHIP, TUMBLING END OVER END, FAR BEHIND.

SOON...
WE DID IT! WE ESCAPED!
WE HAVE THESE GREAT POWERS!
AND WE BEAT THE SNARKS!
HERE, JACK! SEE IF YOU CAN CONDENSE INTO YOUR CLOTHES.
THANKS! DON'T TELL FRIDAY, BUT WHITEY WASN'T A VERY GOOD FIGHTER, WAS HE? AGAINST US, THOSE SNARKS DIDN'T HAVE A CHANCE!
HOLY COW! NOW THAT WE HAVE POWERS WE OUGHT TO HAVE NAMES--LIKE THE HULK... AND SPIDER-MAN!
GEE!
THAT'S IT! I'M GEE! I CONTROL GRAVITY--G POWER! GET IT?
AND I'LL BE LIGHTSPEED, 'CAUSE I FLY REALLY FAST AND LEAVE A TRAIL OF COLORED LIGHT BEHIND ME!
ALEX SAYS I STORE ENERGY LIKE A BATTERY, SO I GET TO BE THE ENERGIZER!
AND JACK'S JACK-IN-THE-BOX, 'CAUSE HE POPS UP AND DOWN LIKE ONE!
NO WAY, PUNK! I'M MASS-MASTER! AND DON'T YOU FORGET IT!
AND ALL TOGETHER--
--WE'RE THE POWER PACK!
YEAH!
WHILE I WAS IN THE SHIP, I SAW A DOOR WITH LOTS OF GUARDS! I'M SURE THAT'S WHERE THEY'RE KEEPING MOM AND DAD!
I KNOW I CAN FIND IT AGAIN IF WE CAN GET INSIDE!
GREAT! WE KNOW WHERE THE SNARKS ARE! WE GOT POWERS! LET'S GO GET THEM BACK!
LOOK, I WANT THEM BACK AS MUCH AS YOU DO...BUT WE CAN'T!
THEY'RE TESTING DAD'S ANTI-MATTER CONVERTER IN ABOUT FOUR HOURS. WE'VE GOT TO STOP IT, OR IT'LL DESTROY THE WORLD!
THAT'S WHY WHITEY DIED--AND GAVE US HIS POWERS!
ALEX, I WANT MY MOMMY, PLEEEASE! I'M SCARED!
I WANT TO GO HOME!

ButterFingers
I WANT MY MOMMY! I WANT TO GO HOME!
WRITTEN BY: LOUISE SIMONSON
PENCILED BY: JUNE BRIGMAN
INKED BY: BOB WIACEK
LETTERED BY: JOE ROSEN
COLORED BY: GLYNIS WEIN
EDITED BY: CARL POTTS
EDITOR IN CHIEF: JIM SHOOTER
NO, KATIE! THOSE ALIEN SNARKS HAVE CAPTURED MOM AND DAD, AND THEY'LL BE WATCHING OUR HOUSE, HOPING THEY CAN GET US, TOO!
AND IN A FEW HOURS, DAD'S BOSS, MR. CARMODY, IS TESTING DAD'S MATTER/ ANTI-MATTER CONVERTER, REMEMBER?
JULIE'S RIGHT, BABY! WE'VE GOT TO STOP HIM, OR HE'LL START A CHAIN REACTION THAT'LL DESTROY THE EARTH!
THAT'S WHY WHITEY CAME TO US FROM OUTER SPACE AND GAVE US OUR POWERS-- AND HIS SMARTSHIP, FRIDAY!
SAVE YOUR BREATH, ALEX! IF WE IGNORE THE BRAT'S TANTRUM, SHE'LL GET OVER IT FAST ENOUGH!

WE CAN'T IGNORE HER WHEN SHE'S LIKE THIS, JACK! SHE'S THE ENERGIZER NOW... A HUMAN BATTERY!
SHE ABSORBED LOTS OF ENERGY EARLIER*AND-- YOW! WATCH IT! SHE'S SHOOTING OFF SPARKS LIKE CRAZY! THIS IS SOME TANTRUM!
*LAST ISSUE.
YOU CALL THOSE SPARKS?
SHRAKK!
YOW!
KATIE, DARN IT! YOU JUST BLASTED FRIDAY!
YEAH! AND LOOK AT THE GRASS BURN! WHAT IF THE SNARKS SEE IT AND INVESTIGATE?
I'LL USE MY GEE POWERS TO FLOAT HER UP INTO THE CLOUDS WHERE SHE CAN'T DO ANY MORE DAMAGE! YOU TWO PUT OUT THE FIRE!
NOW I'VE DONE IT! I CAN CANCEL GRAVITY AND PUSH UP, BUT THEN I CAN'T STOP! I JUST KEEP GOING!
HELP?
ALEX LOOKS LIKE HE'S IN TROUBLE! I'VE GOT TO GET TO THEM WHILE KATIE'S STILL SPARKING! OTHERWISE, I'LL NEVER FIND THEM THROUGH THE CLOUDS! JACK, YOU PUT OUT THE FIRE!
HOW?
DON'T ASK ME! I'M TERRIBLE AT SCIENCE! SMOTHER IT OR SOME-THING!
SMOTHER IT? GIVE ME A BREAK! WITH WHAT?

WAIT A MINUTE! I'M THE MASS-MASTER! MAYBE I CAN SMOTHER IT!
WHAT IF I USE MY DENSITY POWERS TO MOVE MY BODY'S MOLECULES FAR APART SO I BECOME A GAS...
...THEN SETTLE DOWN ON TOP OF THE FIRE...
...AND MOVE THEM CLOSER AND CLOSER TOGETHER SO I GET DENSER...
...AND DENSER ...HEY, I'M GETTING WARM...
...AND DENSER ...YOW! THAT'S HOT!
JACK PANICS... AND INSTANTANEOUSLY DISPERSES HIS BODY'S MOLECULES, BECOMING, ONCE AGAIN, A HUGE, GASEOUS CLOUD.
FWOOOOM!
SECONDS LATER, HE RETURNS TO NORMAL...
HEY, WHEN I WENT CLOUDY REAL FAST, THE FIRE WENT OUT! WHAT HAPPENED?
AND WHY IS IT THAT WHEN I GO CLOUDY, I ALWAYS LOSE MY CLOTHES?
MEANWHILE, IN THE SKY ABOVE...
ALEX! ALEX! WHERE ARE YOU? KATIE'S STOPPED SPARKING AND I CAN'T SEE YOU!
JULIE! JACK! CAN YOU HEAR ME?
WE'RE UP HERE!

BOY, ARE WE GLAD TO SEE YOU!
KATIE, ARE YOU ALL RIGHT?
I-I'M FINE NOW, JULIE! I'M GLAD YOU CAME TO GET US! I WAS SCARED WE'D FLOAT OFF INTO OUTER SPACE AND DIE!
YEAH, ME TOO! I CAN INCREASE MY GRAVITATIONAL PULL **TOWARD** THE EARTH, JULIE, BUT I WAS AFRAID TO EXPERIMENT THIS HIGH UP UNLESS I HAD TO!
WHAT IF WE FELL TOO FAST AND COULDN'T STOP?
DON'T EVEN SAY IT! **SPLAT!** YOU'D NEED A PANCAKE FLIPPER TO GET YOU OFF THE GROUND!
ALEX! JULIE! LOOK! I PUT OUT THE FIRE ALL BY MYSELF!
I BLANKETED THE FIRE IN MY CLOUD FORM AND GOT DENSER AND DENSER TILL IT WAS SO HOT THE FIRE BURNED ME!
THEN I WOOSHED BACK INTO CLOUD FORM, AND LOOK WHAT HAPPENED!
YOUR MOLECULES MUST HAVE RUSHED AWAY FROM THE FIRE SO FAST THAT YOU TOOK ALL THE AIR WITH YOU.
I'LL BET YOU CREATED A VACUUM AROUND THE FIRE, AND FLAMES CAN'T BURN IN A VACUUM. THAT WAS PRETTY SMART!
YEAH? **YEAH!** NOT LIKE THAT DUMB STUNT **KATIE** PULLED!
JUST LOOK AT WHAT YOUR FIRE-BALLS DID TO OUR SMARTSHIP!
OH, NO!
4

I'M SORRY, FRIDAY! I DIDN'T MEAN TO HURT YOU!
NO PERMANENT DAMAGE DONE, KATIE, BUT YOUR BLAST DESTROYED SOME VITAL CIRCUITS. I CAME VERY CLOSE TO BEING A DUMB-SHIP!
OH, FRIDAY, DON'T TEASE ME! PLEASE! AND YOU WON'T TELL DADDY, WILL YOU? WHEN SOMETHING HAPPENS TO THE CIRCUITS ON HIS COMPUTER AT WORK, HE GETS REAL MAD!
AND YOU'RE MUCH MORE IMPORTANT THAN AN OLD COMPUTER!
THANK YOU, KATIE. DO NOT WORRY. YOUR FATHER NEED NEVER KNOW!
I AM REBUILDING THEM AS RAPIDLY AS POSSIBLE, AND BY NOON TOMORROW, I WILL BE AS GOOD AS NEW.
NOON! WE HAVE TO LEAVE FOR DAD'S LAB LONG BEFORE THEN!
WE DON'T EVEN KNOW WHERE IT IS, AND WE CAN'T GET THERE NOW, ANYWAY! WITHOUT FRIDAY, WE'RE SUNK! BOY, THIS TIME KATIE REALLY BLEW IT!
ACTUALLY, I KNOW HOW TO GET US THERE, IF FRIDAY CAN TELL US WHERE TO GO!
BUT EVEN IF WE GET THERE, JACK WON'T BE ABLE TO DO ANYTHING, 'CAUSE EVERY TIME HE SWITCHES TO CLOUD FORM, HIS CLOTHES FALL OFF!
I'LL BET WHITEY MADE HIS POWERS WORK THAT WAY ON PURPOSE 'CAUSE JACK'S SO MEAN!
I DOUBT THAT, KATIE! IT IS SIMPLY THAT IN HIS GASEOUS STATE, SOLID OBJECTS PASS RIGHT THROUGH HIM.
BUT I HAVE PRESENTS HERE FOR ALL OF YOU, WITH SPECIAL PROPERTIES THAT WILL MAKE JACK'S LIFE MUCH EASIER!
WOW! COSTUMES! SUPER-HERO COSTUMES!
OOH! MINE'S ROSE, LIKE THE INSIDE OF MY RAIN-BOW WHEN I'M LIGHT-SPEED!
LOOK AT THE SPECIAL SYMBOLS FOR OUR POWERS! MINE SHOWS CON-TROL OVER AN OBJECT'S GRAVITY!
AND LITTLE SILVER BOOTIES! ISN'T THAT SWEET?... FOR A GIRL? I THINK THIS IS A SISSY SUIT!
HEY, JACK, WHY DON'T YOU JUST SHUT UP!
5

"SISSY SUIT" OR NOT, JACK, IT IS WOVEN OF UNSTABLE MOLECULES AND WILL BECOME SOLID OR GAS AS YOU DO!
BESIDE KATIE, I HAVE PLACED A MAP OF THE AREA AND HAVE MARKED THE ROUTE TO THE LAB! WE ARE A LITTLE OVER A HUNDRED MILES AWAY!
THANKS! WE'LL NEED DAD'S BLUEPRINTS, TOO, SO WE CAN RECOGNIZE THE CONVERTER WHEN WE SEE IT! AT THE RATE JULIE FLIES, EVEN PUSHING US, WE SHOULD BE THERE WELL BEFORE DAWN!
SO THAT'S YOUR PLAN!
I DON'T KNOW IF I CAN LAST TILL DAWN! I'M STARVING! FRIDAY, HAVE YOU GOT ANYTHING TO EAT?
TRY SOME OF THIS! IT WAS WHITEY'S FAVORITE!
UGH! BLUE SAWDUST!
UH, GEE, FRIDAY! THAT LOOKS GREAT BUT, UH, WE REALLY BETTER GET GOING!
YEAH, FRIDAY! THANKS FOR THE MAP! WE'LL BE BACK SOON!
LATER...
WE'RE NOT LOST, ARE WE, ALEX?
I HOPE NOT! THE WIND'S WHIPPING THE MAP AROUND SO MUCH I CAN HARDLY READ IT! I THINK IT'S GOING TO RAIN!
SWELL! HOW CAN KATIE SLEEP THROUGH ALL THIS?
HEY! THERE'S A BIG BOY RESTAURANT UP AHEAD! MAYBE WE SHOULD STOP THERE AND ASK DIRECTIONS!
YEAH! MAYBE WE'D LOOK SO PATHETIC THEY'D FEED US...FOR FREE!
I WISH WE HAD SOME MONEY FOR FOOD!
NO KIDDING! WE SURE CAN'T EAT THAT BLUE STUFF FRIDAY OFFERED US! AND I, FOR ONE, COULD EAT ALMOST ANYTHING!
IF WE CAN'T BUY FOOD THEN WE'LL JUST HAVE TO STEAL IT!
WE CAN'T, JACK! IT ISN'T HONEST!
I JUST WISH I'D BROUGHT A BOOK ALONG! IF I WAS READING, I WOULDN'T REALIZE HOW HUNGRY I WAS!
IT'S TOO DARK TO READ, ANYWAY! I JUST HOPE WE'RE FOLLOWING THE RIGHT ROAD!
I JUST HOPE IT DOESN'T RAIN!

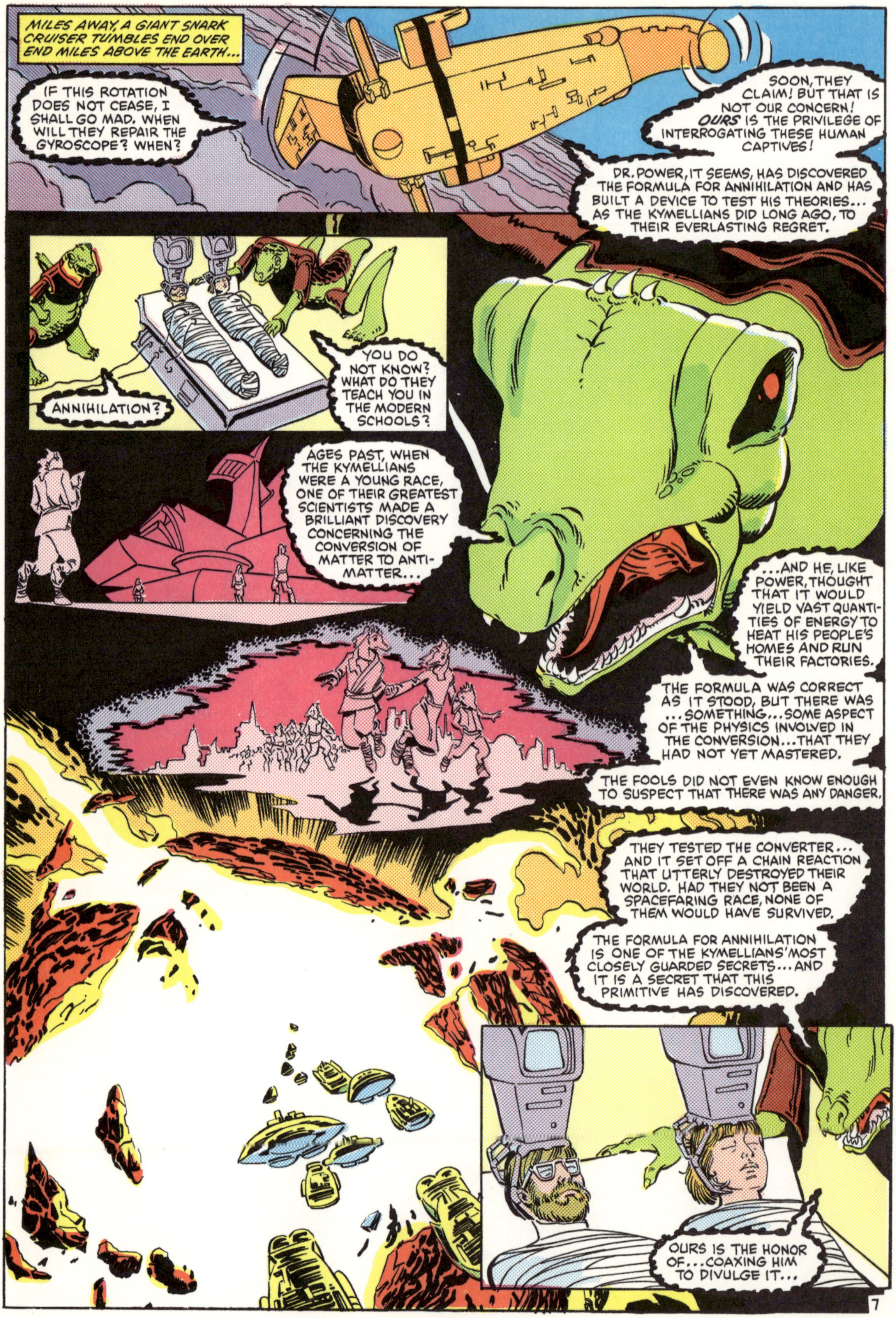
MILES AWAY, A GIANT SNARK CRUISER TUMBLES END OVER END MILES ABOVE THE EARTH...
IF THIS ROTATION DOES NOT CEASE, I SHALL GO MAD. WHEN WILL THEY REPAIR THE GYROSCOPE? WHEN?
SOON, THEY CLAIM! BUT THAT IS NOT OUR CONCERN! OURS IS THE PRIVILEGE OF INTERROGATING THESE HUMAN CAPTIVES!
DR. POWER, IT SEEMS, HAS DISCOVERED THE FORMULA FOR ANNIHILATION AND HAS BUILT A DEVICE TO TEST HIS THEORIES... AS THE KYMELLIANS DID LONG AGO, TO THEIR EVERLASTING REGRET.
ANNIHILATION?
YOU DO NOT KNOW? WHAT DO THEY TEACH YOU IN THE MODERN SCHOOLS?
AGES PAST, WHEN THE KYMELLIANS WERE A YOUNG RACE, ONE OF THEIR GREATEST SCIENTISTS MADE A BRILLIANT DISCOVERY CONCERNING THE CONVERSION OF MATTER TO ANTI-MATTER...
...AND HE, LIKE POWER, THOUGHT THAT IT WOULD YIELD VAST QUANTITIES OF ENERGY TO HEAT HIS PEOPLE'S HOMES AND RUN THEIR FACTORIES.
THE FORMULA WAS CORRECT AS IT STOOD, BUT THERE WAS ...SOMETHING...SOME ASPECT OF THE PHYSICS INVOLVED IN THE CONVERSION...THAT THEY HAD NOT YET MASTERED.
THE FOOLS DID NOT EVEN KNOW ENOUGH TO SUSPECT THAT THERE WAS ANY DANGER.
THEY TESTED THE CONVERTER... AND IT SET OFF A CHAIN REACTION THAT UTTERLY DESTROYED THEIR WORLD. HAD THEY NOT BEEN A SPACEFARING RACE, NONE OF THEM WOULD HAVE SURVIVED.
THE FORMULA FOR ANNIHILATION IS ONE OF THE KYMELLIANS' MOST CLOSELY GUARDED SECRETS... AND IT IS A SECRET THAT THIS PRIMITIVE HAS DISCOVERED.
OURS IS THE HONOR OF...COAXING HIM TO DIVULGE IT...

THANK THE EGG! FINALLY THE GYRO-SCOPE IS REPAIRED! I COULD NOT HAVE TAKEN MUCH MORE SPINNING AROUND!
WHO WOULD HAVE THOUGHT THAT A KYMELLIAN SORCERER COULD GIVE HIS POWERS TO FOUR EARTH CHILDREN...
...OR THAT THEY, ALONE, COULD EXTENSIVE-LY DAMAGE OUR SHIP! GYROSCOPE, RADAR, ENERGY FEED LINES--ALL DESTROYED!
AND BY THE TIME THE SHIP IS FULLY OPER-ATIONAL, THE CAPTAIN EXPECTS US TO HAVE THE LOCATION OF THE MATTER-ANTI-MATTER CONVERTER FROM DR. POWER!
AND SEDATED AS THEY ARE, BOTH POWER AND HIS WIFE ARE PROVING INCREDI-BLY RESISTANT TO OUR MIND PROBES! THE HUMANS, IT APPEARS, ARE A STUB-BORN RACE!
THEN OUR GLORY WILL BE THAT MUCH GREATER WHEN WE BREAK THEM!
MEANWHILE...
HEY, WE MADE IT! THERE'S DAD'S LAB! I CAN'T BELIEVE IT! KATIE, BABY! WAKE UP! WE'RE HERE!
THERE'RE AN AWFUL LOT OF BUILDINGS--IT'S A BIG RESEARCH FACILITY! WE DON'T EVEN KNOW WHICH ONE DAD'S CONVERTER MACHINE IS IN.
JUST PICK A ROOF! ANY ROOF! MY ARMS ARE KILLING ME! I WANT TO REST!
SEEMS AS GOOD A PLAN AS ANY! HERE GOES--
HAOOOGA
WHAT WAS THAT?
WE MUST HAVE TRIPPED SOME KIND OF BURGLAR ALARM! WHAT'RE WE GONNA DO?
LET'S GET OUTTA HERE!
WE CAN'T, JULIE! THE CONVERTER IS HERE SOMEWHERE! WE GOTTA FIND IT!

YOU'RE THE BRAIN, ALEX! THINK OF SOMETHING! I CAN HEAR PEOPLE COMING!
ALL RIGHT! I DO HAVE AN IDEA!
JACK, GO CLOUDY! SO DENSE YOU MAKE A REAL PEA-SOUP FOG. I DON'T WANT THE GUYS COMING UP THOSE STAIRS TO SEE ANYTHING!
YOU GIRLS GET BEHIND THE SHED...
...WHILE I GET ON TOP! HERE THEY COME!
...FIND WHATEVER SET OFF THOSE ALARMS! AND IF IT'S ANOTHER GOL-DURN PIGEON, STRANGLE IT!
YES, SIR!
BOY, CARMODY'S REALLY CRAZED TONIGHT!
IT'S THAT TEST TOMORROW! IT'S GOT HIM-- URK!
OOF!
NOW, JACK! GO SOLID AND GET INSIDE! QUICK! ALL OF YOU!
AND SHUT THE DOOR BEHIND US!
SLAM!
HEY! WHAT WAS THAT?
I DON'T KNOW, BUT IT GOT OUR WALKIE-TALKIE!
HURRY, JULIE, CLOSE THE BOLT! THEY'RE TRYING TO HAMMER THE DOOR OPEN! I'M GLAD THEY DON'T HAVE GUNS!
BAM! BAM!
THIS IS CARMODY! REPORT IN! WHAT'S GOING ON UP THERE?
UH-OH!
HEY, DON'T WORRY! I KNOW HOW TO HANDLE THIS! I SAW IT IN A MOVIE!
...UH...ROGER...UH...EVERYTHING'S OKAY HERE...JUST RAN INTO TECHNICAL DIFFICULTIES, SIR...JUST A PIGEON!
WHAT'S GOING ON?!? WHO IS THIS??!?
SOUNDS PRETTY MAD. MAYBE YOU'D BETTER DISINTEGRATE THIS, KATIE!
I SAW STAR WARS, TOO, DUMMY. IT DIDN'T WORK FOR HAN SOLO, EITHER!
9

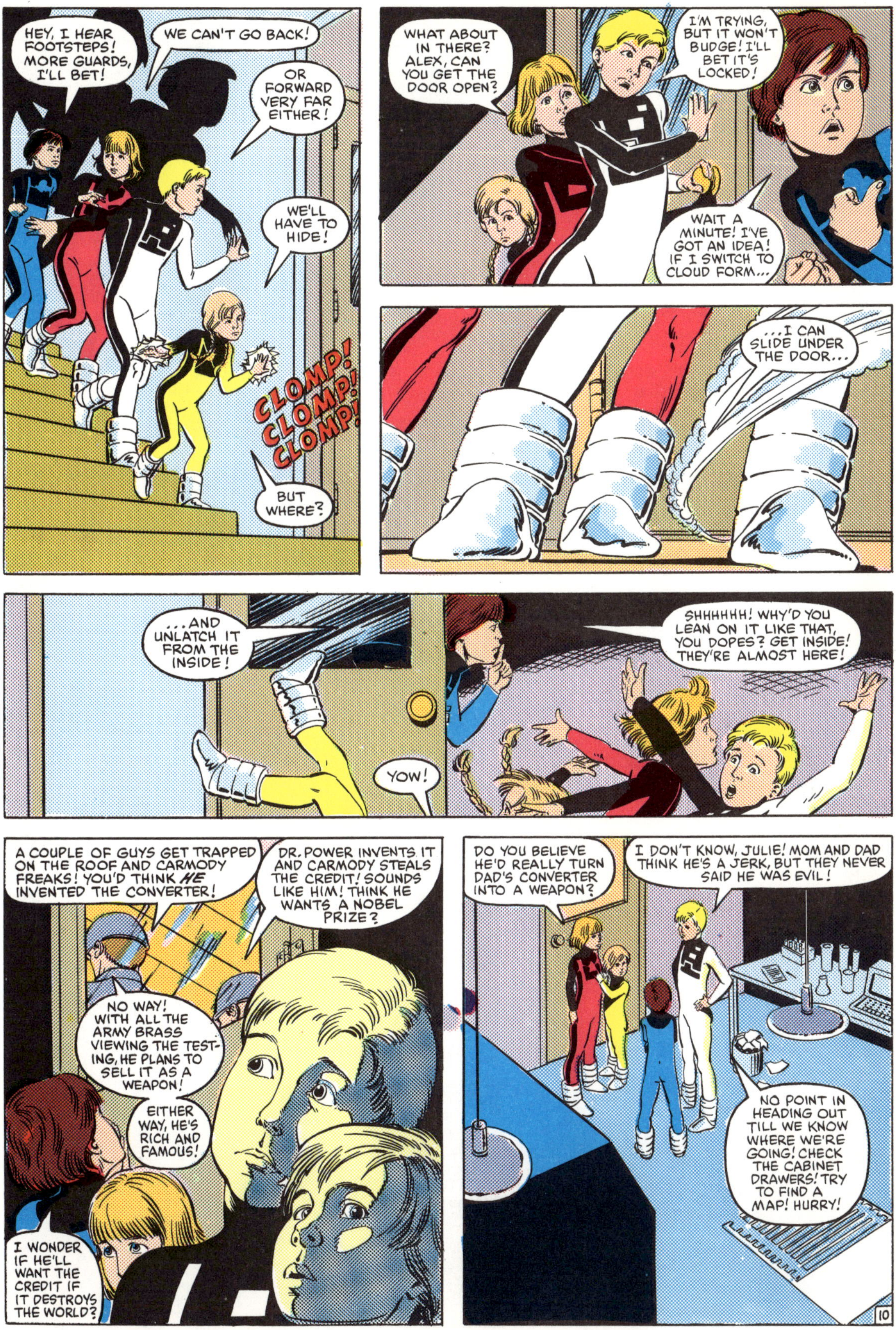
HEY, I HEAR FOOTSTEPS! MORE GUARDS, I'LL BET!
WE CAN'T GO BACK!
OR FORWARD VERY FAR EITHER!
WE'LL HAVE TO HIDE!
CLOMP! CLOMP! CLOMP!
BUT WHERE?
WHAT ABOUT IN THERE? ALEX, CAN YOU GET THE DOOR OPEN?
I'M TRYING, BUT IT WON'T BUDGE! I'LL BET IT'S LOCKED!
WAIT A MINUTE! I'VE GOT AN IDEA! IF I SWITCH TO CLOUD FORM...
...I CAN SLIDE UNDER THE DOOR...
...AND UNLATCH IT FROM THE INSIDE!
YOW!
SHHHHHH! WHY'D YOU LEAN ON IT LIKE THAT, YOU DOPES? GET INSIDE! THEY'RE ALMOST HERE!
A COUPLE OF GUYS GET TRAPPED ON THE ROOF AND CARMODY FREAKS! YOU'D THINK HE INVENTED THE CONVERTER!
DR. POWER INVENTS IT AND CARMODY STEALS THE CREDIT! SOUNDS LIKE HIM! THINK HE WANTS A NOBEL PRIZE?
NO WAY! WITH ALL THE ARMY BRASS VIEWING THE TESTING, HE PLANS TO SELL IT AS A WEAPON!
EITHER WAY, HE'S RICH AND FAMOUS!
I WONDER IF HE'LL WANT THE CREDIT IF IT DESTROYS THE WORLD?
DO YOU BELIEVE HE'D REALLY TURN DAD'S CONVERTER INTO A WEAPON?
I DON'T KNOW, JULIE! MOM AND DAD THINK HE'S A JERK, BUT THEY NEVER SAID HE WAS EVIL!
NO POINT IN HEADING OUT TILL WE KNOW WHERE WE'RE GOING! CHECK THE CABINET DRAWERS! TRY TO FIND A MAP! HURRY!
10

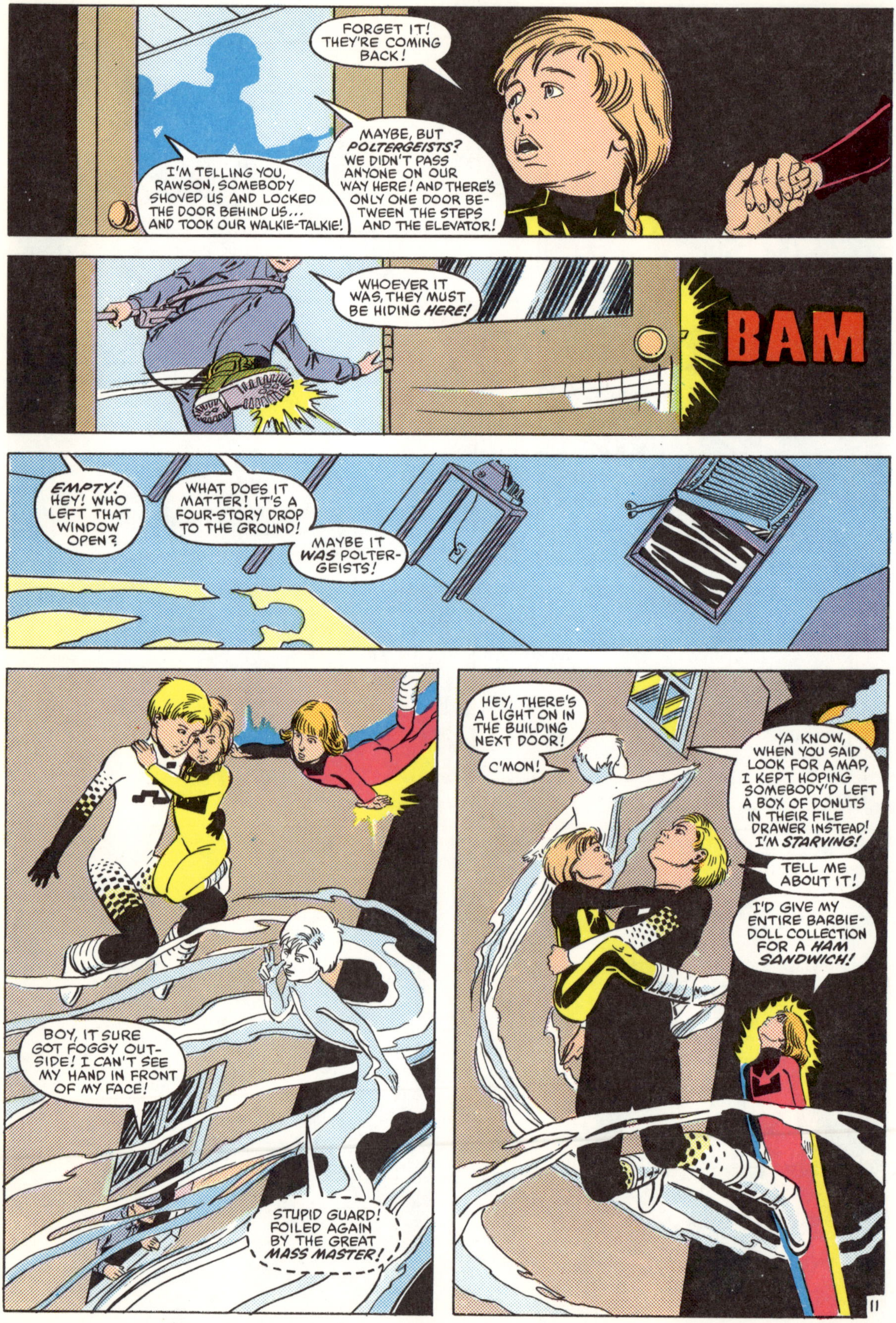
FORGET IT! THEY'RE COMING BACK!
I'M TELLING YOU, RAWSON, SOMEBODY SHOVED US AND LOCKED THE DOOR BEHIND US... AND TOOK OUR WALKIE-TALKIE!
MAYBE, BUT POLTERGEISTS? WE DIDN'T PASS ANYONE ON OUR WAY HERE! AND THERE'S ONLY ONE DOOR BETWEEN THE STEPS AND THE ELEVATOR!
WHOEVER IT WAS, THEY MUST BE HIDING HERE!
BAM
EMPTY! HEY! WHO LEFT THAT WINDOW OPEN?
WHAT DOES IT MATTER! IT'S A FOUR-STORY DROP TO THE GROUND!
MAYBE IT WAS POLTERGEISTS!
BOY, IT SURE GOT FOGGY OUTSIDE! I CAN'T SEE MY HAND IN FRONT OF MY FACE!
STUPID GUARD! FOILED AGAIN BY THE GREAT MASS MASTER!
HEY, THERE'S A LIGHT ON IN THE BUILDING NEXT DOOR!
C'MON!
YA KNOW, WHEN YOU SAID LOOK FOR A MAP, I KEPT HOPING SOMEBODY'D LEFT A BOX OF DONUTS IN THEIR FILE DRAWER INSTEAD! I'M STARVING!
TELL ME ABOUT IT!
I'D GIVE MY ENTIRE BARBIE-DOLL COLLECTION FOR A HAM SANDWICH!

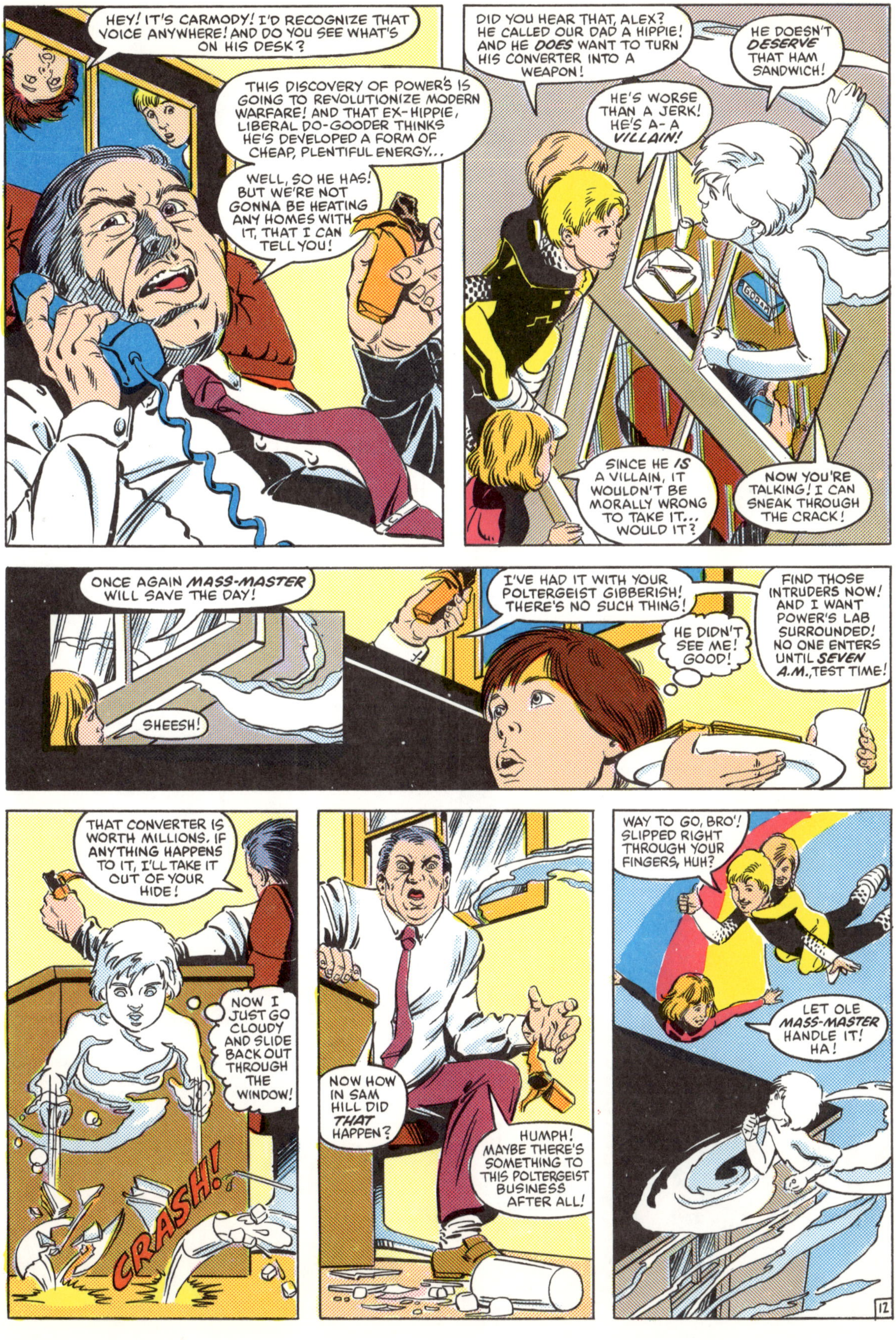
HEY! IT'S CARMODY! I'D RECOGNIZE THAT VOICE ANYWHERE! AND DO YOU SEE WHAT'S ON HIS DESK?
THIS DISCOVERY OF POWER'S IS GOING TO REVOLUTIONIZE MODERN WARFARE! AND THAT EX-HIPPIE, LIBERAL DO-GOODER THINKS HE'S DEVELOPED A FORM OF CHEAP, PLENTIFUL ENERGY...
WELL, SO HE HAS! BUT WE'RE NOT GONNA BE HEATING ANY HOMES WITH IT, THAT I CAN TELL YOU!
DID YOU HEAR THAT, ALEX? HE CALLED OUR DAD A HIPPIE! AND HE DOES WANT TO TURN HIS CONVERTER INTO A WEAPON!
HE DOESN'T DESERVE THAT HAM SANDWICH!
HE'S WORSE THAN A JERK! HE'S A- A VILLAIN!
SINCE HE IS A VILLAIN, IT WOULDN'T BE MORALLY WRONG TO TAKE IT... WOULD IT?
NOW YOU'RE TALKING! I CAN SNEAK THROUGH THE CRACK!
ONCE AGAIN MASS-MASTER WILL SAVE THE DAY!
SHEESH!
I'VE HAD IT WITH YOUR POLTERGEIST GIBBERISH! THERE'S NO SUCH THING!
HE DIDN'T SEE ME! GOOD!
FIND THOSE INTRUDERS NOW! AND I WANT POWER'S LAB SURROUNDED! NO ONE ENTERS UNTIL SEVEN A.M., TEST TIME!
THAT CONVERTER IS WORTH MILLIONS. IF ANYTHING HAPPENS TO IT, I'LL TAKE IT OUT OF YOUR HIDE!
NOW I JUST GO CLOUDY AND SLIDE BACK OUT THROUGH THE WINDOW!
CRASH!
NOW HOW IN SAM HILL DID THAT HAPPEN?
HUMPH! MAYBE THERE'S SOMETHING TO THIS POLTERGEIST BUSINESS AFTER ALL!
WAY TO GO, BRO'! SLIPPED RIGHT THROUGH YOUR FINGERS, HUH?
LET OLE MASS-MASTER HANDLE IT! HA!
12

MINUTES LATER...
OKAY, JULIE. WE ARE HIGH ENOUGH TO SEE!
HIGH ENOUGH TO SEE WHAT?
CARMODY ORDERED THE TEST BUILDING SURROUNDED! IF WE FOLLOW THE GUARDS, WE'LL FIND IT IN NO TIME!
SMART! THERE IT IS!
JACK, GIVE US SOME COVER!
I WONDER WHAT TIME IT IS. IT'S GETTING LIGHTER!
AND WINDIER! I'M HAVING TROUBLE STAYING TOGETHER! IF THOSE GUARDS DON'T SPOT US, THEY'RE EVEN DUMBER THAN THEY LOOK!
ALEX, HOW'LL WE GET INSIDE?
THAT'S YOUR JOB, KATIE! SEE THAT WINDOW? THINK YOU CAN DISINTEGRATE THE GLASS?
SURE!
MEANWHILE...
INCREASE THE STRENGTH OF THE MIND PROBE? BUT, SIR, THIS CRUISER'S FACILITIES ARE PRIMITIVE! THEIR BRAINS MIGHT BE DAMAGED!
NOW THAT OUR SHIP IS OPERATIONAL, OUGHT WE NOT RETURN TO OUR MOTHERSHIP AS ORDERED AND LET THEM INTERROGATE THE PRISONERS?
OUR QUEEN MOTHER IS ALREADY FURIOUS AT OUR DELAY AND THE DAMAGES WE INCURRED!
DO AS I SAY, DOLT! HER FURY WILL TURN TO GLEE... WHEN WE BRING HER, NOT A FORMULA, BUT THE CONVERTER/ANNIHILATOR ITSELF!
RRR
RZZ
NNN
THE CONVERTER, DR. POWER! WHERE IS IT? WHERE?
...UNGH... LAB... LAB!

HOLY COW!
DAD BUILT *THAT?*
IT'S *GIGANTIC!*
KATIE'LL *NEVER* BE ABLE TO DISINTEGRATE IT!
I COULD DO *PART* OF IT!
BUT WE DON'T KNOW WHICH PART IS IMPORTANT!
SO OLD SMART-ALEX, READ THE BLUEPRINTS!
I DON'T KNOW HOW-- AT LEAST NOT ONES THIS COMPLEX! I WOULDN'T KNOW WHERE TO BEGIN!
THEN WE'LL *NEVER* BE ABLE TO DO IT!
WHITEY DIED... SO WE COULD HAVE HIS POWER AND USE IT TO DESTROY THIS CONVERTER AND SAVE OUR WORLD!
IT WAS STUPID OF HIM! WE'RE JUST KIDS, JULIE! WE DON'T KNOW ANYTHING ABOUT IT!
MAYBE WE SHOULD JUST TELL CARMODY!
THAT VILLAIN! YOU HEARD HIM! HE'S CRAZY! BESIDES, HE WOULDN'T LISTEN TO A BUNCH OF KIDS!
NO! *WE* WERE GIVEN THESE POWERS! *WE'VE* GOT TO STOP HIM! IT'S UP TO US!
AT LEAST WE'VE GOT TO TRY, ALEX!
YOU'RE RIGHT. AND THERE'S ONLY ONE THING WE CAN DO! IF WE CAN'T DESTROY IT, WE'LL HAVE TO TAKE IT WITH US!
YOU'RE NUTS! YOU DON'T EVEN KNOW IF YOUR GRAVITY POWERS WILL WORK ON SOMETHING THAT BIG!
14

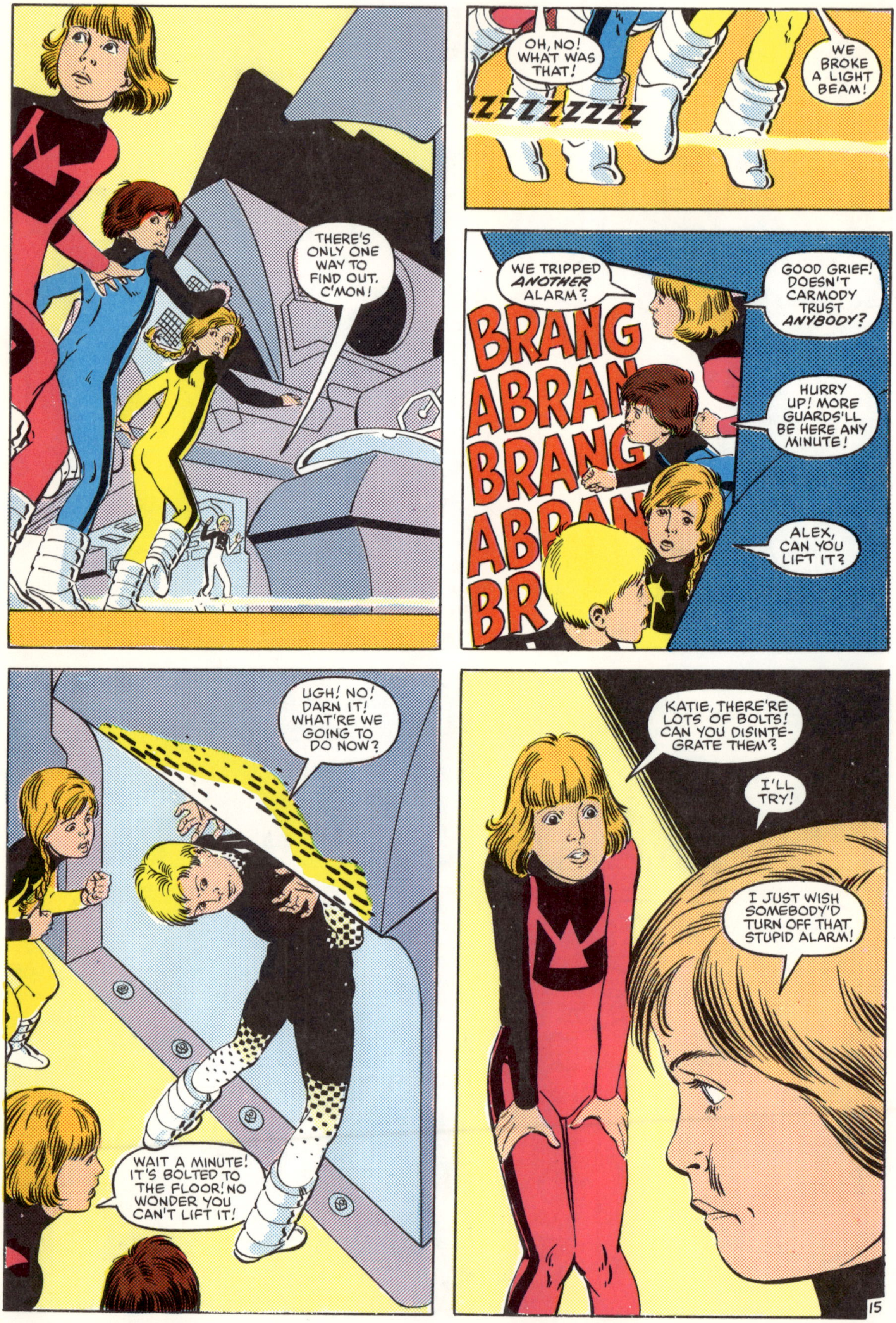

THERE'S ONLY ONE WAY TO FIND OUT. C'MON!
OH, NO! WHAT WAS THAT!
ZZZZZZZZZ
WE BROKE A LIGHT BEAM!
WE TRIPPED ANOTHER ALARM?
BRANG ABRAN BRANG ABRAN BR
GOOD GRIEF! DOESN'T CARMODY TRUST ANYBODY?
HURRY UP! MORE GUARDS'LL BE HERE ANY MINUTE!
ALEX, CAN YOU LIFT IT?
UGH! NO! DARN IT! WHAT'RE WE GOING TO DO NOW?
WAIT A MINUTE! IT'S BOLTED TO THE FLOOR! NO WONDER YOU CAN'T LIFT IT!
KATIE, THERE'RE LOTS OF BOLTS! CAN YOU DISINTEGRATE THEM?
I'LL TRY!
I JUST WISH SOMEBODY'D TURN OFF THAT STUPID ALARM!

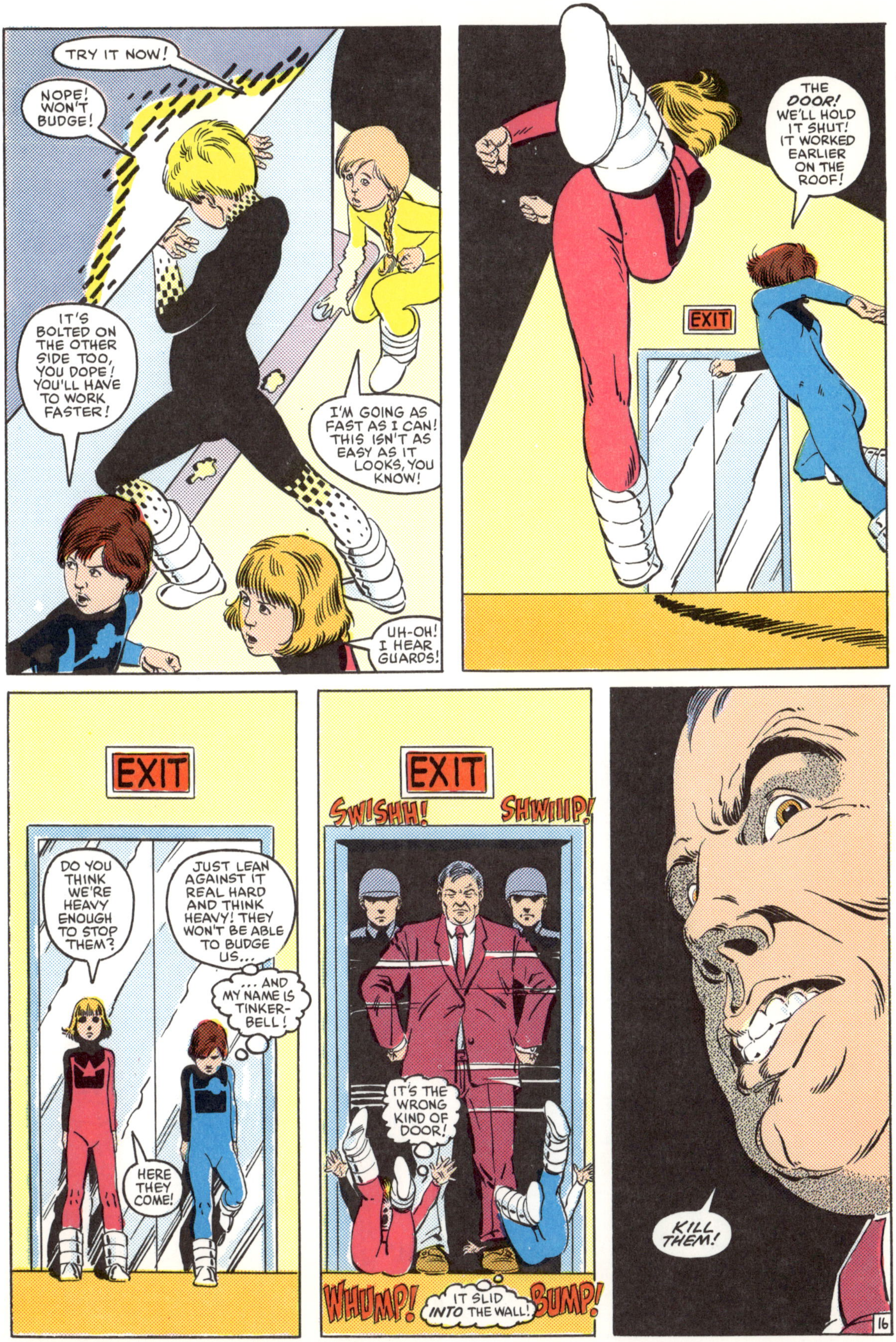
TRY IT NOW!
NOPE! WON'T BUDGE!
IT'S BOLTED ON THE OTHER SIDE TOO, YOU DOPE! YOU'LL HAVE TO WORK FASTER!
I'M GOING AS FAST AS I CAN! THIS ISN'T AS EASY AS IT LOOKS, YOU KNOW!
UH-OH! I HEAR GUARDS!
THE *DOOR!* WE'LL HOLD IT SHUT! IT WORKED EARLIER ON THE ROOF!
EXIT
EXIT
DO YOU THINK WE'RE HEAVY ENOUGH TO STOP THEM?
JUST LEAN AGAINST IT REAL HARD AND THINK HEAVY! THEY WON'T BE ABLE TO BUDGE US...
... AND MY NAME IS TINKER-BELL!
HERE THEY COME!
EXIT
SWISHH!
SHWIIIP!
IT'S THE WRONG KIND OF DOOR!
WHUMP!
IT SLID *INTO* THE WALL!
BUMP!
KILL THEM!

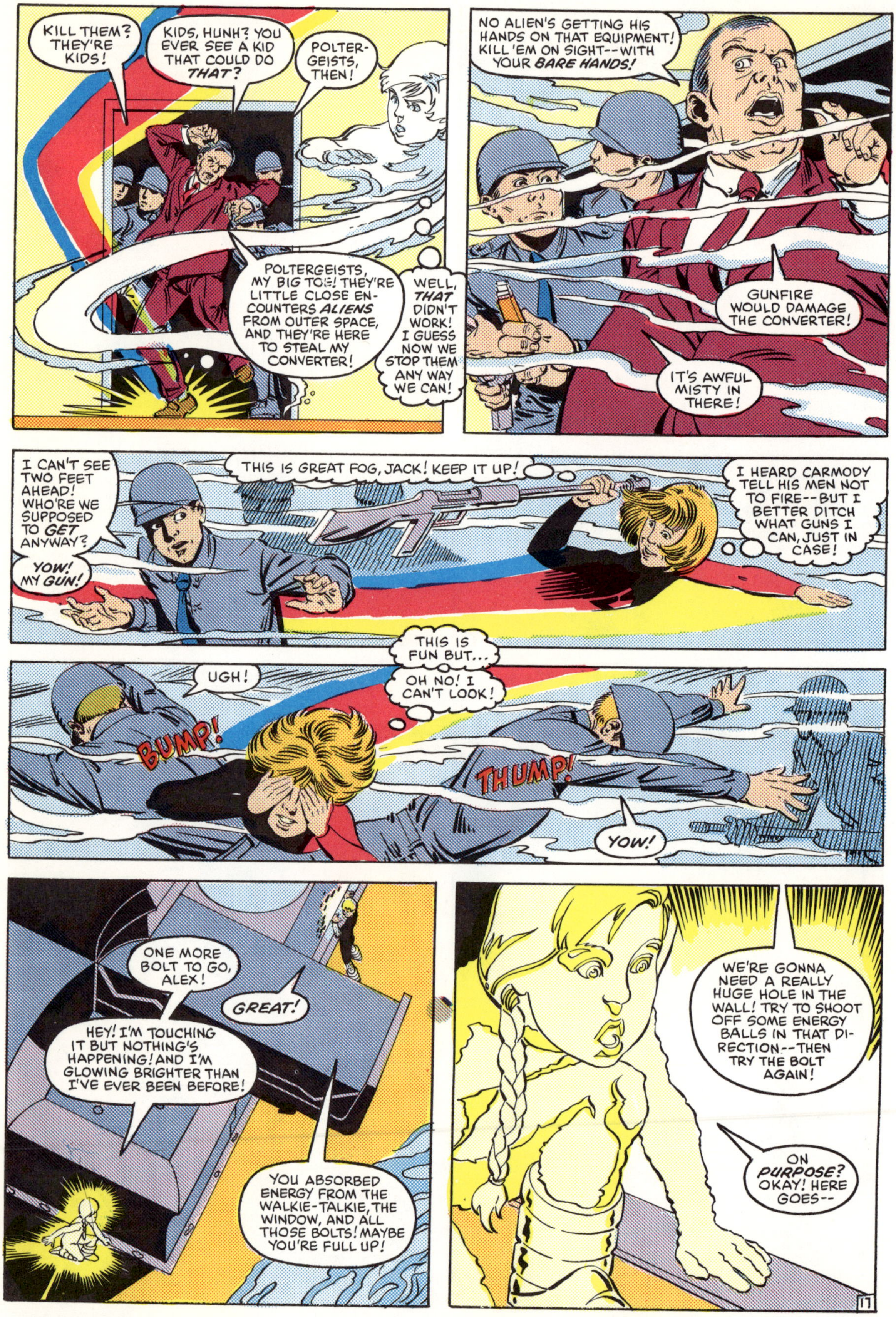

KILL THEM? THEY'RE KIDS!
KIDS, HUNH? YOU EVER SEE A KID THAT COULD DO *THAT?*
POLTER-GEISTS, THEN!
POLTERGEISTS, MY BIG TOE! THEY'RE LITTLE CLOSE EN-COUNTERS *ALIENS* FROM OUTER SPACE, AND THEY'RE HERE TO STEAL MY CONVERTER!
WELL, *THAT* DIDN'T WORK! I GUESS NOW WE STOP THEM ANY WAY WE CAN!
NO ALIEN'S GETTING HIS HANDS ON THAT EQUIPMENT! KILL 'EM ON SIGHT--WITH YOUR *BARE HANDS!*
GUNFIRE WOULD DAMAGE THE CONVERTER!
IT'S AWFUL MISTY IN THERE!
I CAN'T SEE TWO FEET AHEAD! WHO'RE WE SUPPOSED TO *GET* ANYWAY?
YOW! MY *GUN!*
THIS IS GREAT FOG, JACK! KEEP IT UP!
I HEARD CARMODY TELL HIS MEN NOT TO FIRE--BUT I BETTER DITCH WHAT GUNS I CAN, JUST IN CASE!
UGH!
BUMP!
THIS IS FUN BUT...
OH NO! I CAN'T LOOK!
THUMP!
YOW!
ONE MORE BOLT TO GO, ALEX!
GREAT!
HEY! I'M TOUCHING IT BUT NOTHING'S HAPPENING! AND I'M GLOWING BRIGHTER THAN I'VE EVER BEEN BEFORE!
YOU ABSORBED ENERGY FROM THE WALKIE-TALKIE, THE WINDOW, AND ALL THOSE BOLTS! MAYBE YOU'RE FULL UP!
WE'RE GONNA NEED A REALLY HUGE HOLE IN THE WALL! TRY TO SHOOT OFF SOME ENERGY BALLS IN THAT DI-RECTION--THEN TRY THE BOLT AGAIN!
ON *PURPOSE?* OKAY! HERE GOES--

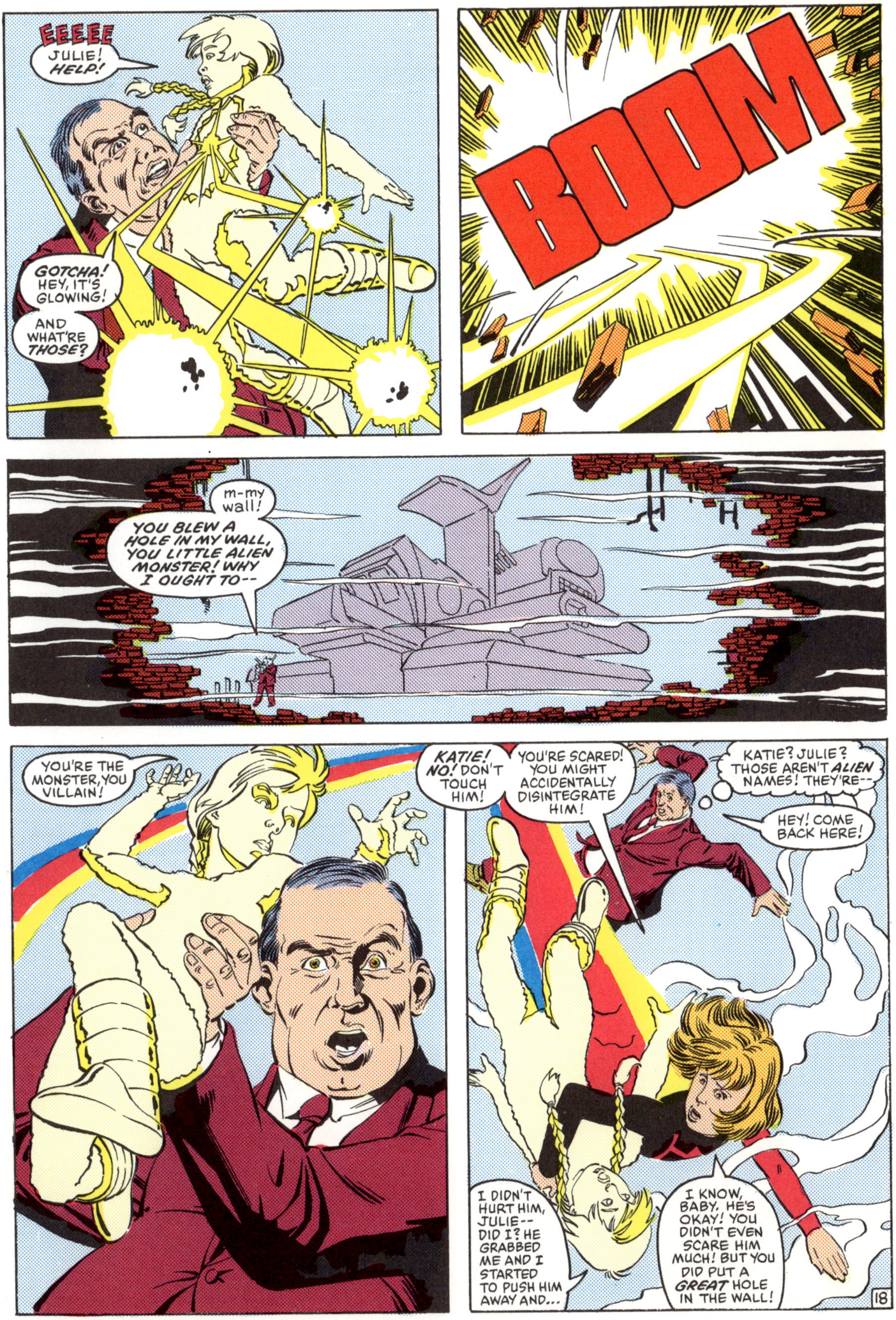
EEEEE
JULIE! HELP!
GOTCHA! HEY, IT'S GLOWING!
AND WHAT'RE THOSE?
BOOM
m-my wall!
YOU BLEW A HOLE IN MY WALL, YOU LITTLE ALIEN MONSTER! WHY I OUGHT TO--
YOU'RE THE MONSTER, YOU VILLAIN!
KATIE! NO! DON'T TOUCH HIM!
YOU'RE SCARED! YOU MIGHT ACCIDENTALLY DISINTEGRATE HIM!
KATIE? JULIE? THOSE AREN'T ALIEN NAMES! THEY'RE--
HEY! COME BACK HERE!
I DIDN'T HURT HIM, JULIE-- DID I? HE GRABBED ME AND I STARTED TO PUSH HIM AWAY AND...
I KNOW, BABY. HE'S OKAY! YOU DIDN'T EVEN SCARE HIM MUCH! BUT YOU DID PUT A GREAT HOLE IN THE WALL!

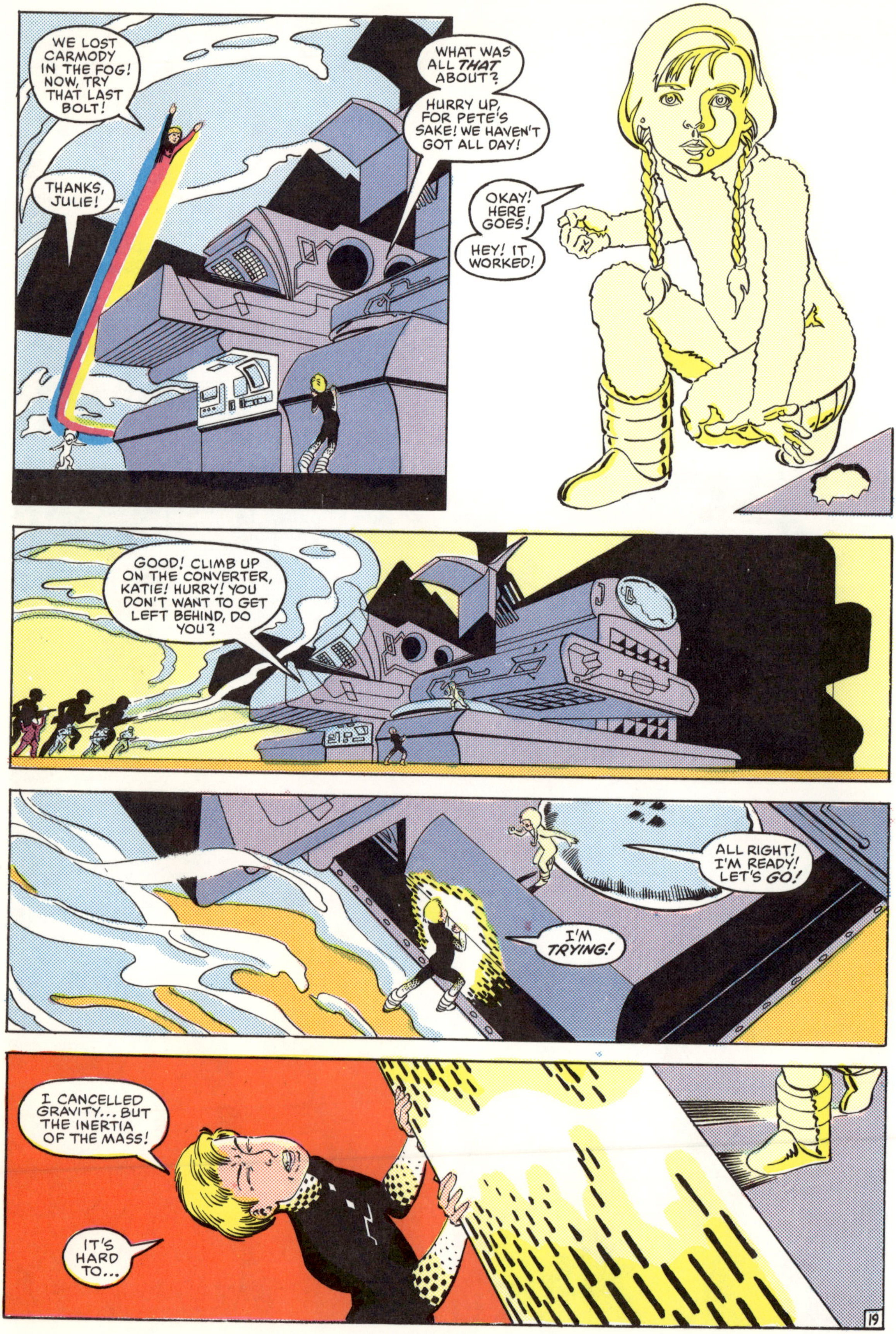

WE LOST CARMODY IN THE FOG! NOW, TRY THAT LAST BOLT!
THANKS, JULIE!
WHAT WAS ALL *THAT* ABOUT?
HURRY UP, FOR PETE'S SAKE! WE HAVEN'T GOT ALL DAY!
OKAY! HERE GOES!
HEY! IT WORKED!
GOOD! CLIMB UP ON THE CONVERTER, KATIE! HURRY! YOU DON'T WANT TO GET LEFT BEHIND, DO YOU?
ALL RIGHT! I'M READY! LET'S *GO!*
I'M *TRYING!*
I CANCELLED GRAVITY... BUT THE INERTIA OF THE MASS!
IT'S HARD TO...

...SHIFT...
HEY! YOU DID IT! I FELT IT LIFT A LITTLE!
JUST GOT TO PUSH US OFF IN THE RIGHT DIRECTION!
HANG ON... HERE GOES NOTHING!
THERE'S SOMETHING BIG --MOVING IN THE MIST! IT CAN'T BE! I DON'T BELIEVE IT!
WHEEEEEEEE!
LET'S GET THIS SHOW ON THE ROAD, OKAY?
THOSE GUARDS BACK THERE HAVE GUNS, EVEN IF, FOR SOME REASON, THEY'RE STILL NOT USING THEM!
THEY AREN'T SHOOTING BE-CAUSE THEY CAN'T SEE WHERE *TO* SHOOT, DUMMY! THE GREAT MASS-MASTER IS STILL OBSCURING THEIR VISION!
OR SHOULD I SAY THE GREAT *WIMP!* MAKING FOG AND SNEAKING THROUGH CRACKS IS ALL I'M *GOOD* FOR!
WHEN IT COMES TO SOMETHING IMPORTANT, LIKE THAT FIGHT BACK THERE, MY POWER'S A TOTAL WASTE!

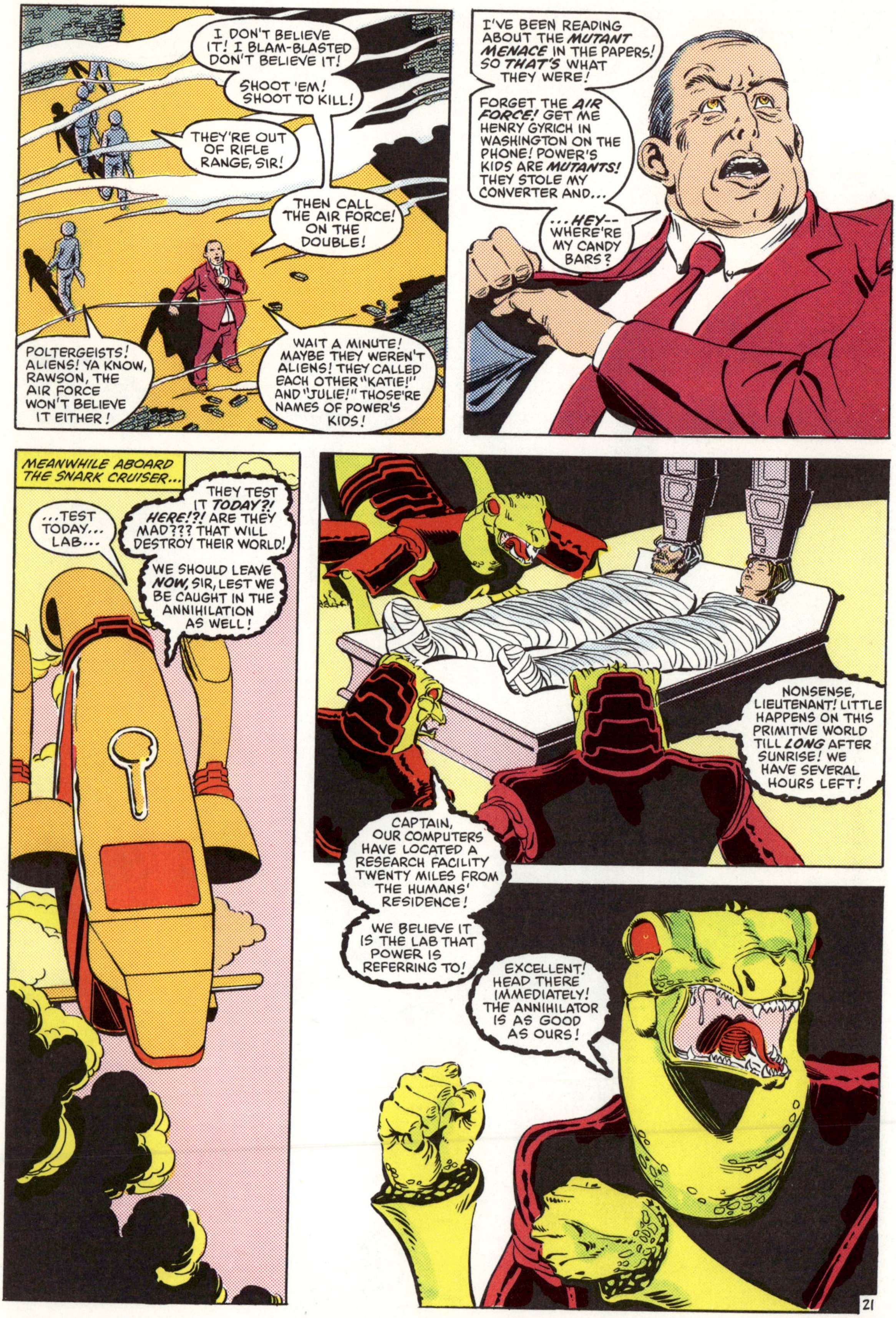
I DON'T BELIEVE IT! I BLAM-BLASTED DON'T BELIEVE IT!
SHOOT 'EM! SHOOT TO KILL!
THEY'RE OUT OF RIFLE RANGE, SIR!
THEN CALL THE AIR FORCE! ON THE DOUBLE!
POLTERGEISTS! ALIENS! YA KNOW, RAWSON, THE AIR FORCE WON'T BELIEVE IT EITHER!
WAIT A MINUTE! MAYBE THEY WEREN'T ALIENS! THEY CALLED EACH OTHER "KATIE!" AND "JULIE!" THOSE'RE NAMES OF POWER'S KIDS!
I'VE BEEN READING ABOUT THE MUTANT MENACE IN THE PAPERS! SO THAT'S WHAT THEY WERE!
FORGET THE AIR FORCE! GET ME HENRY GYRICH IN WASHINGTON ON THE PHONE! POWER'S KIDS ARE MUTANTS! THEY STOLE MY CONVERTER AND...
...HEY-- WHERE'RE MY CANDY BARS?
MEANWHILE ABOARD THE SNARK CRUISER...
...TEST TODAY... LAB...
THEY TEST IT TODAY?! HERE!?! ARE THEY MAD??? THAT WILL DESTROY THEIR WORLD!
WE SHOULD LEAVE NOW, SIR, LEST WE BE CAUGHT IN THE ANNIHILATION AS WELL!
NONSENSE, LIEUTENANT! LITTLE HAPPENS ON THIS PRIMITIVE WORLD TILL LONG AFTER SUNRISE! WE HAVE SEVERAL HOURS LEFT!
CAPTAIN, OUR COMPUTERS HAVE LOCATED A RESEARCH FACILITY TWENTY MILES FROM THE HUMANS' RESIDENCE!
WE BELIEVE IT IS THE LAB THAT POWER IS REFERRING TO!
EXCELLENT! HEAD THERE IMMEDIATELY! THE ANNIHILATOR IS AS GOOD AS OURS!

MEANWHILE...
IT CAN'T BE GETTING WINDIER, CAN IT?
ALL I KNOW IS THAT NOW THAT WE'RE FAR FROM THE LAB, I DON'T EVEN HAVE TO PUSH, ANYMORE!
THE WIND IS SAILING THIS THING ALONG LIKE A GIANT KITE!
WHERE'RE WE TAKING IT, ANYWAY? I DON'T SEE ANY PLACE TO PUT IT DOWN!
ME NEITHER!
HEY, YOU GUYS! QUIT WIGGLING, UP THERE! JUST BECAUSE THIS CONVERTER DOESN'T WEIGH ANYTHING, DOESN'T MEAN IT'S EASY TO BALANCE!
IT ISN'T US, ALEX! IT'S THE WIND!
WHATEVER IT IS, IT'S-- WHOA!
OH, NO! THE WIND JERKED IT OUT OF MY HANDS! MY GRAVITY POWERS AREN'T AFFECTING THE MACHINE ANY MORE!
WHICH MEANS...
JULIEEEEEEE
GOT YA!
CRR-ASSH!
22

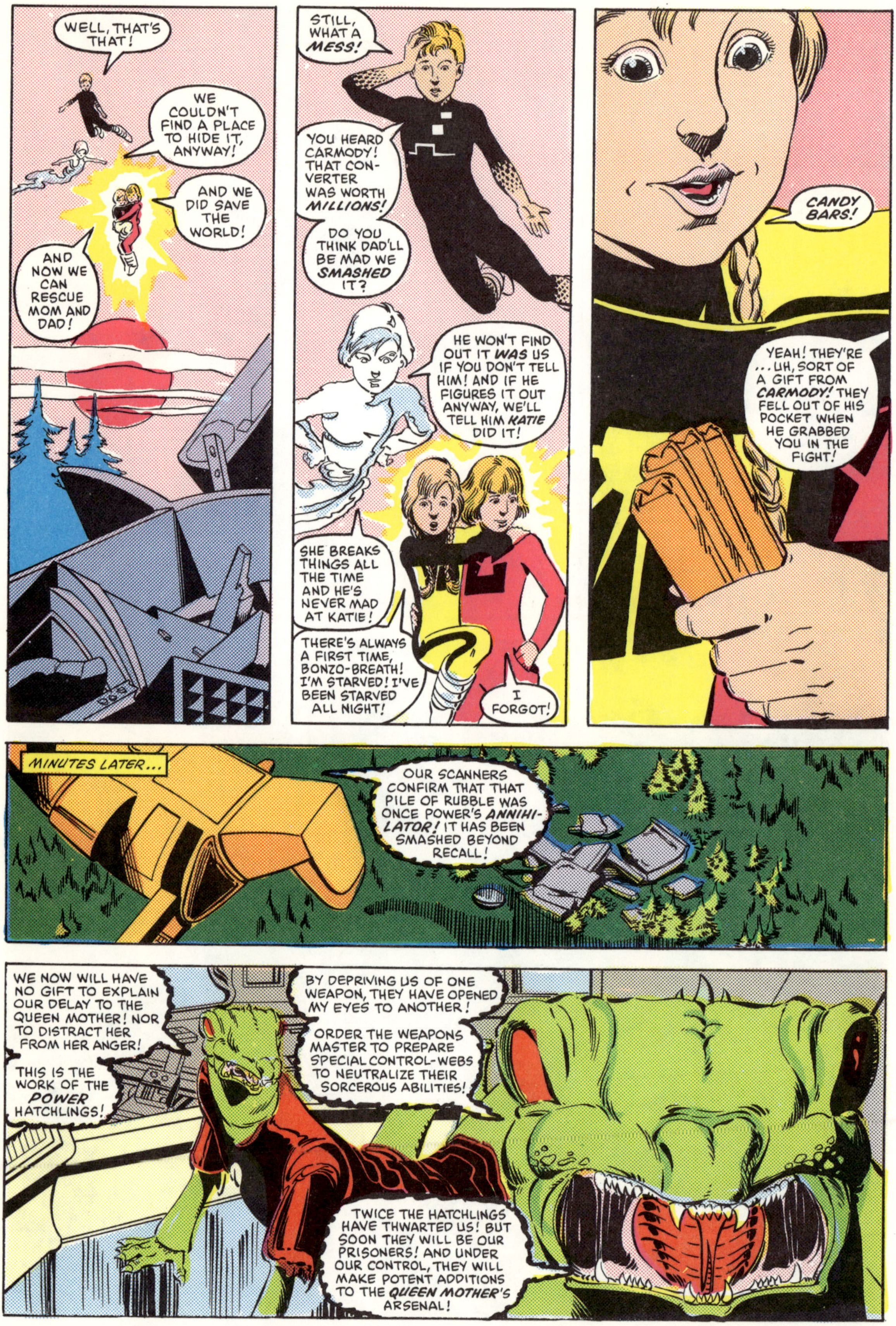
WELL, THAT'S THAT!
WE COULDN'T FIND A PLACE TO HIDE IT, ANYWAY!
AND WE DID SAVE THE WORLD!
AND NOW WE CAN RESCUE MOM AND DAD!
STILL, WHAT A MESS!
YOU HEARD CARMODY! THAT CONVERTER WAS WORTH MILLIONS!
DO YOU THINK DAD'LL BE MAD WE SMASHED IT?
HE WON'T FIND OUT IT WAS US IF YOU DON'T TELL HIM! AND IF HE FIGURES IT OUT ANYWAY, WE'LL TELL HIM KATIE DID IT!
SHE BREAKS THINGS ALL THE TIME AND HE'S NEVER MAD AT KATIE!
THERE'S ALWAYS A FIRST TIME, BONZO-BREATH! I'M STARVED! I'VE BEEN STARVED ALL NIGHT!
I FORGOT!
CANDY BARS!
YEAH! THEY'RE ...UH, SORT OF A GIFT FROM CARMODY! THEY FELL OUT OF HIS POCKET WHEN HE GRABBED YOU IN THE FIGHT!
MINUTES LATER...
OUR SCANNERS CONFIRM THAT THAT PILE OF RUBBLE WAS ONCE POWER'S ANNIHILATOR! IT HAS BEEN SMASHED BEYOND RECALL!
WE NOW WILL HAVE NO GIFT TO EXPLAIN OUR DELAY TO THE QUEEN MOTHER! NOR TO DISTRACT HER FROM HER ANGER!
THIS IS THE WORK OF THE POWER HATCHLINGS!
BY DEPRIVING US OF ONE WEAPON, THEY HAVE OPENED MY EYES TO ANOTHER!
ORDER THE WEAPONS MASTER TO PREPARE SPECIAL CONTROL-WEBS TO NEUTRALIZE THEIR SORCEROUS ABILITIES!
TWICE THE HATCHLINGS HAVE THWARTED US! BUT SOON THEY WILL BE OUR PRISONERS! AND UNDER OUR CONTROL, THEY WILL MAKE POTENT ADDITIONS TO THE QUEEN MOTHER'S ARSENAL!

LOUISE SIMONSON WRITER
JUNE BRIGMAN PENCILER
BOB WIACEK INKER
JOE ROSEN LETTERS
GLYNIS WEIN COLORS
CARL POTTS EDITOR
JIM SHOOTER EDITOR-IN-CHIEF
KIDNAPPED!
I CAN'T BELIEVE IT! WE ACTUALLY USED THE POWERS WHITEY GAVE US TO DESTROY THE ANNIHILATOR DAD INVENTED BEFORE IT COULD EXPLODE THE WORLD!
SWELL! AND NOW WE RESCUE MOM AND DAD... ASSUMING THE SNARKS HAVEN'T CARRIED THEM OFF TO THEIR PLANET BY NOW! WE'VE WASTED ENOUGH TIME!
WASTED--? WHY, JACK POWER! IF WE HADN'T STOPPED THE TEST WE WOULDN'T BE HERE TO RESCUE ANYBODY!
WHITEY DIED TRYING TO HELP US--
GIVE IT A BREAK, JULIE! JACK KNOWS THAT. HE'S TIRED AND GROUCHY --WE ALL ARE!
GROUCHIER! I HAVE TO STAY IN MY CLOUD FORM TO HIDE YOU GUYS IN CASE THE SNARKS SHOW UP!
YOUR GRAVITY POWERS DON'T STOP YOU FROM EATING! JULIE'S LIGHTSPEED POWERS DON'T STOP HER! NEITHER DO KATIE'S ENERGY POWERS!
BUT ME? I'M STARVING AND CLOUDS CAN'T EAT!

YOU POOR OL' MASS-MASTER! WE WILL FIND MOM AND DAD! BUT HOW?
SIMPLE, PEA-BRAIN! WE FIND THE SNARKS!
YEAH! FRIDAY'S RADAR CAN LOCATE THEIR SHIP IN NO TIME!
IF IT'S WORKING! LOTS OF HER CIRCUITS BROKE WHEN MY ENERGY BALL HIT HER LAST NIGHT!
ALEX...DO BROKEN CIRCUITS FEEL ANY-THING LIKE A LOOSE TOOTH?
WHILE MILES AWAY...
ELECTRICAL CIRCUITS REPAIRED, AT LAST! ANTI-GRAVITY PODS OPERATIONAL! SOON I SHALL BE ABLE TO FLY!
RADAR WILL TAKE LONGER! FOR A SMALL GIRL, KATIE IS QUITE DESTRUC-TIVE. AT LEAST SHE WAS EQUALLY HARD ON THE SNARKS.
THEY SEEMED MOST UPSET BY THE DAMAGE SHE DID TO THEIR CRUISER! WHERE IS SHE ANYWAY? WHERE ARE THEY ALL?
THIS WORLD STILL EXISTS, WHICH PROVES THEY HAVE DESTROYED THE ANNIHILATOR! SO WHY HAVE THEY NOT RETURNED?
RRRMMMM...MM!
THE SNARKS!
< SCANNERS INDICATE THAT THE KYMELLIAN SMARTSHIP FRIDAY... >
< ...REGISTERED TO THE SORCERER AELFYRE WHITEMANE, HAS BEEN DISABLED AND ABANDONED BY THE POWER HATCHLINGS. >
< EXCELLENT! >
< S-SIR, WE SAW THE RUINS OF DR. POWER'S ANNIHILATOR... AND THERE ARE RUMORS THAT OUR MIND PROBE DAMAGED HIS MEMORY, AS WELL! >
< IT WILL MEAN OUR HEADS TO RETURN TO THE QUEEN MOTHER WITH A BROKEN SHIP, A DAMAGED CAPTIVE AND OUR MISSION UNFULFILLED! >
2

<NONSENSE, YOU CRETIN! BELOW IS A KYMELLIAN SMARTSHIP-- WHOSE LIKE WE HAVE NEVER CAPTURED! AND SOON POWER'S SORCEROUS CHILDREN WILL BE OURS, AS WELL!>
<EVEN IF POWER WERE DAMAGED, OUR QUEEN MOTHER WOULD FIND THESE GIFTS IRRESISTIBLE AND LAVISH HER FAVOR UPON US!>
<ACTIVATE THE TRACTOR BEAM-- NOW, FOOL-- AND CAPTURE THAT SHIP!>
LATER...
I'M SURE WE CAME THE RIGHT WAY! SO WHERE IS FRIDAY?
WHY ASK ME? YOU HAVE THE MAP...DON'T YOU?
WELL, I DON'T! IF YOU'LL RE-MEMBER, I CAN'T CARRY STUFF IN MY CLOUD FORM!
HEY, DON'T LOOK AT ME!
I DON'T BELIEVE THIS! YOU GUYS ACTU-ALLY LOST THE MAP?
WE'RE NOT TOO FAR FROM OUR HOUSE! WE'RE TIRED AND HUNGRY. MAYBE WE SHOULD JUST GO HOME!
AND WALK INTO A SNARK TRAP? WHAT IF THEY'RE WATCHING THE HOUSE, WAITING FOR US?
WE COULD SNEAK IN UNDER CLOUD COVER!
I'M GAME! WHY NOT? THAT SEEMS TO BE ALL I'M GOOD FOR!

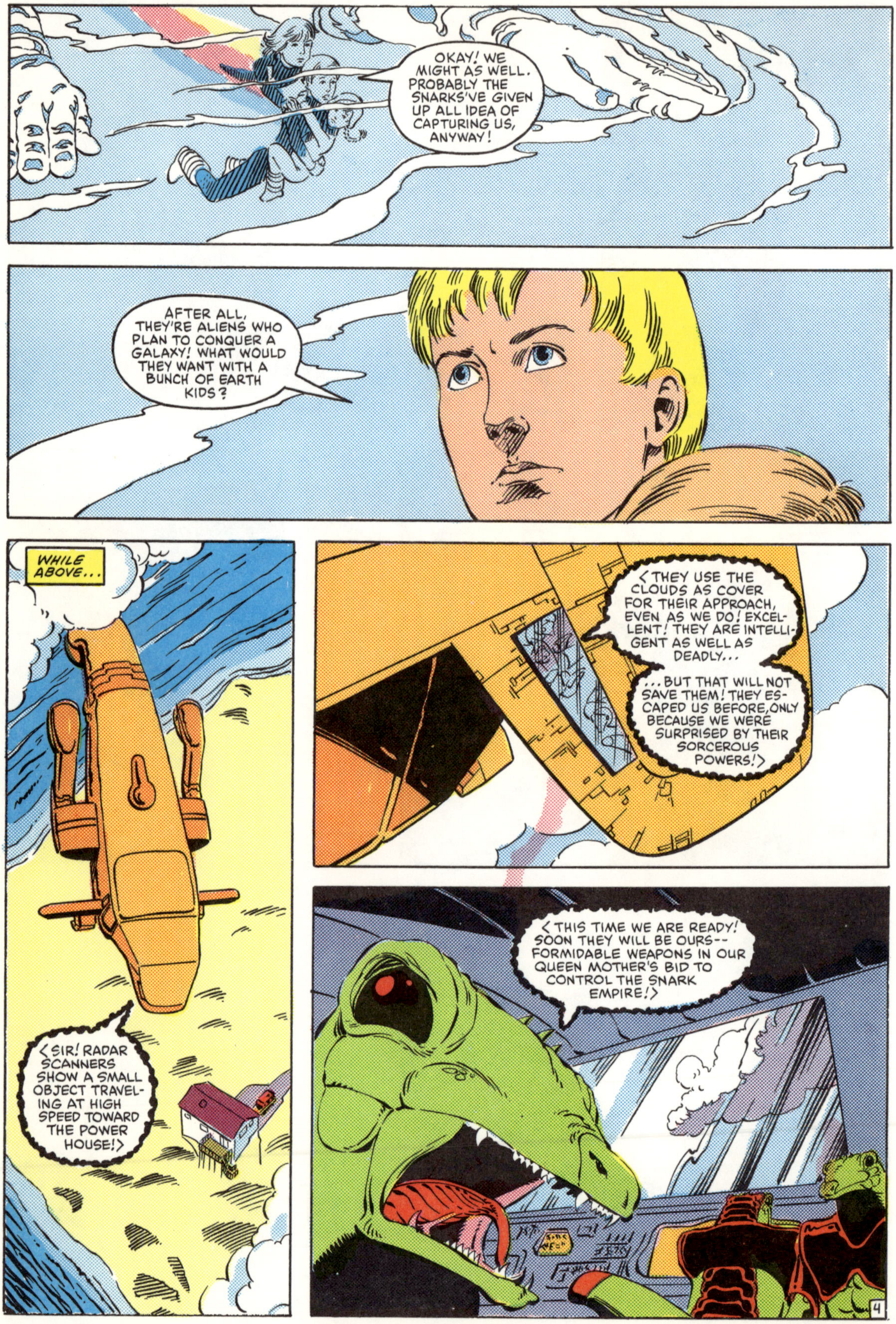
OKAY! WE MIGHT AS WELL. PROBABLY THE SNARKS'VE GIVEN UP ALL IDEA OF CAPTURING US, ANYWAY!
AFTER ALL, THEY'RE ALIENS WHO PLAN TO CONQUER A GALAXY! WHAT WOULD THEY WANT WITH A BUNCH OF EARTH KIDS?
WHILE ABOVE...
<SIR! RADAR SCANNERS SHOW A SMALL OBJECT TRAVELING AT HIGH SPEED TOWARD THE POWER HOUSE!>
<THEY USE THE CLOUDS AS COVER FOR THEIR APPROACH, EVEN AS WE DO! EXCELLENT! THEY ARE INTELLIGENT AS WELL AS DEADLY...
...BUT THAT WILL NOT SAVE THEM! THEY ESCAPED US BEFORE, ONLY BECAUSE WE WERE SURPRISED BY THEIR SORCEROUS POWERS!>
<THIS TIME WE ARE READY! SOON THEY WILL BE OURS-- FORMIDABLE WEAPONS IN OUR QUEEN MOTHER'S BID TO CONTROL THE SNARK EMPIRE!>

WHILE BELOW...
THERE'S OUR HOUSE! I DON'T SEE ANY SNARKS, THOUGH!
GOOD. JUST LAST NIGHT WE WERE ON THE BACK PORCH, WATCHING FOR UFO'S WITH YOUR TELESCOPE! HARD TO BELIEVE, HUH, ALEX?
YEAH! YOU WERE EVEN READING HAVE SPACESUIT, WILL TRAVEL!
AND I SAW FRIDAY FLOATING IN THE WATER AND WE WENT DOWN TO THE BEACH!
THEN THE SNARKS SHOWED UP!
HERE'S WHERE THEY GRABBED US!
OH, NO! MY TELE-SCOPE!
YUCK! SO MUCH FOR GETTING STUFF TO EAT!
5

THEY MUST'VE MADE THIS MESS WHEN THEY CAME LOOKING FOR DAD'S BLUEPRINTS TO THE ANNIHI-LATOR--
JUST FOR FUN!
ALEX...? MY TOOTH IS LOOSER NOW!
I WANT TO TELL MY MOMMY!
DON'T CRY, BABY! WE'LL GET MOMMY BACK! I PROMISE!
LISTEN, I'LL FIND YOU AN APPLE! YOU CAN BITE INTO IT...
...THEN WHEN MOMMY COMES BACK YOUR TOOTH WILL BE REAL LOOSE. WON'T THAT BE NEAT?
GOOD LUCK FINDING THAT APPLE!
HERE'S ONE!
SNIFF
CHOMP
GREAT! THERE'S NOT MUCH ELSE THAT'S EDIBLE. LET'S GATHER WHAT WE CAN AND--
RRRMMMMMMMMMMMMM
SNARKS!
THEY WON'T LET US ESCAPE AND A LOT OF GOOD WE'LL BE TO MOM AND DAD IF WE GET CAPTURED!
WAIT! IN A WAY, WE'VE GOT THEM WHERE WE WANT THEM! THEY'VE COME TO US!
CRASH!
RRRMMMMMMMMMM
WE CAN'T JUST ATTACK THEM, ALEX! WE'LL BE SLAUGHTERED!
JULIE'S RIGHT, BRO! WE NEED A PLAN!

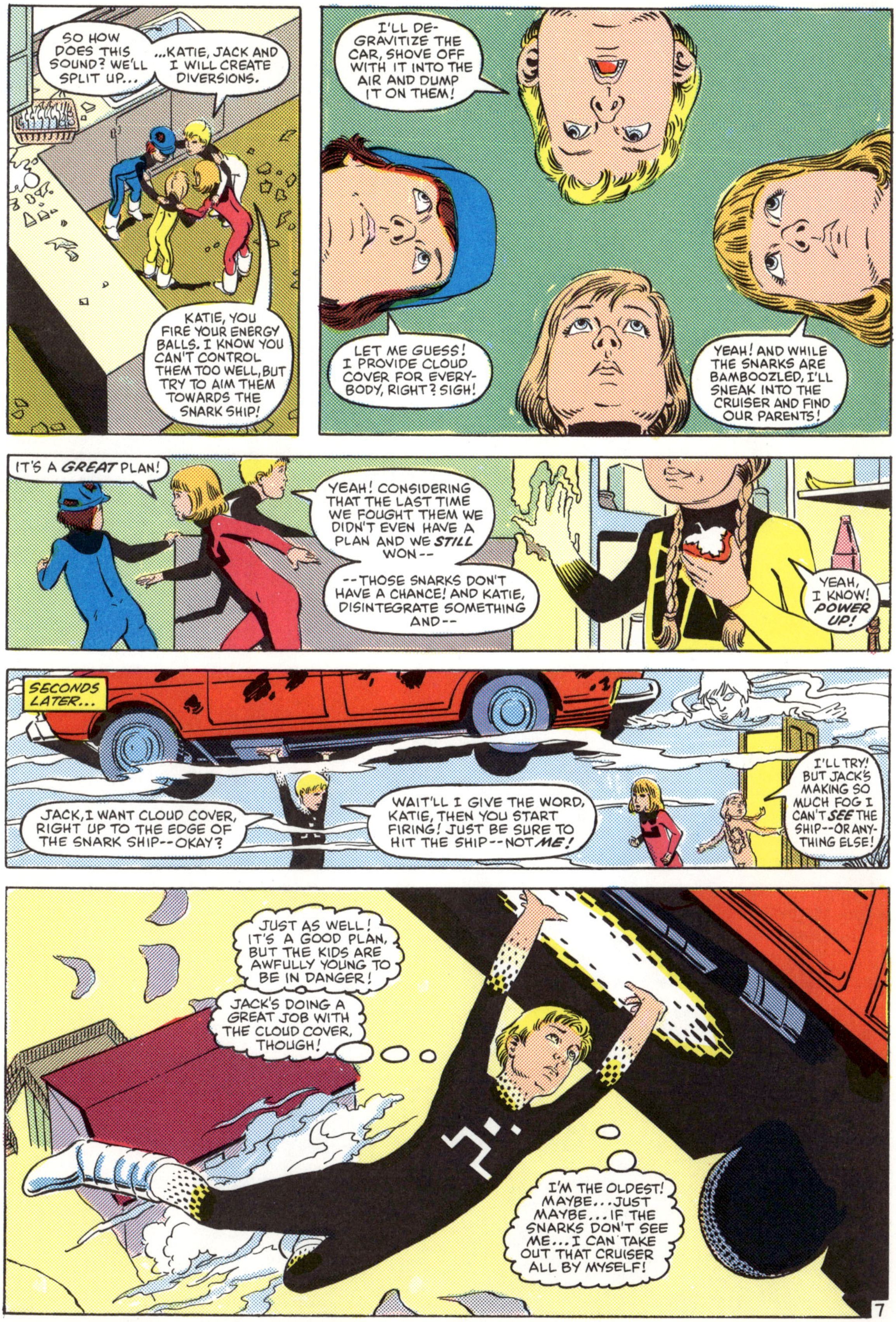

SO HOW DOES THIS SOUND? WE'LL SPLIT UP...
...KATIE, JACK AND I WILL CREATE DIVERSIONS.
KATIE, YOU FIRE YOUR ENERGY BALLS. I KNOW YOU CAN'T CONTROL THEM TOO WELL, BUT TRY TO AIM THEM TOWARDS THE SNARK SHIP!
I'LL DE-GRAVITIZE THE CAR, SHOVE OFF WITH IT INTO THE AIR AND DUMP IT ON THEM!
LET ME GUESS! I PROVIDE CLOUD COVER FOR EVERYBODY, RIGHT? SIGH!
YEAH! AND WHILE THE SNARKS ARE BAMBOOZLED, I'LL SNEAK INTO THE CRUISER AND FIND OUR PARENTS!
IT'S A GREAT PLAN!
YEAH! CONSIDERING THAT THE LAST TIME WE FOUGHT THEM WE DIDN'T EVEN HAVE A PLAN AND WE STILL WON--
--THOSE SNARKS DON'T HAVE A CHANCE! AND KATIE, DISINTEGRATE SOMETHING AND--
YEAH, I KNOW! POWER UP!
SECONDS LATER...
JACK, I WANT CLOUD COVER, RIGHT UP TO THE EDGE OF THE SNARK SHIP--OKAY?
WAIT'LL I GIVE THE WORD, KATIE, THEN YOU START FIRING! JUST BE SURE TO HIT THE SHIP--NOT ME!
I'LL TRY! BUT JACK'S MAKING SO MUCH FOG I CAN'T SEE THE SHIP--OR ANYTHING ELSE!
JUST AS WELL! IT'S A GOOD PLAN, BUT THE KIDS ARE AWFULLY YOUNG TO BE IN DANGER!
JACK'S DOING A GREAT JOB WITH THE CLOUD COVER, THOUGH!
I'M THE OLDEST! MAYBE...JUST MAYBE...IF THE SNARKS DON'T SEE ME...I CAN TAKE OUT THAT CRUISER ALL BY MYSELF!

I'M PAST THE CLOUD COVER NOW! SO FAR, SO GOOD!
<ABOVE US! ONE OF THE HATCHLINGS! THE BOY WHO CANCELS GRAVITY!
FIGHTERS--CAPTURE HIM--BUT GENTLY! IF HE IS SO MUCH AS BRUISED, YOU ANSWER TO ME!>
WHAT ARE THOSE THINGS?
WHO CARES? THEY'RE COMING RIGHT AT ME!
BETTER DUMP THIS WHILE I STILL CAN!
<GET BACK, SIR! HE HAS LAUNCHED A PROJECTILE--
--RIGHT AT THE BRIDGE!>
WOW!
CRASH!
<ELECTRICAL SYSTEMS ...DISRUPTED!>
KA-BOOOM!
<SPARKS... EVERYWHERE! HEAD DOWN, SIR, BEFORE-->
WHOOOM!
UGH!

< HE FALLS-- UNCONSCIOUS...
...AND HE IS OURS!>
< A FORMIDABLE OPPONENT!>
AND BELOW...
OH NO!
JULIE! KATIE! STUFF'S FALLING!
OUT OF THE WAY! RUN!
CRA-KLANG!

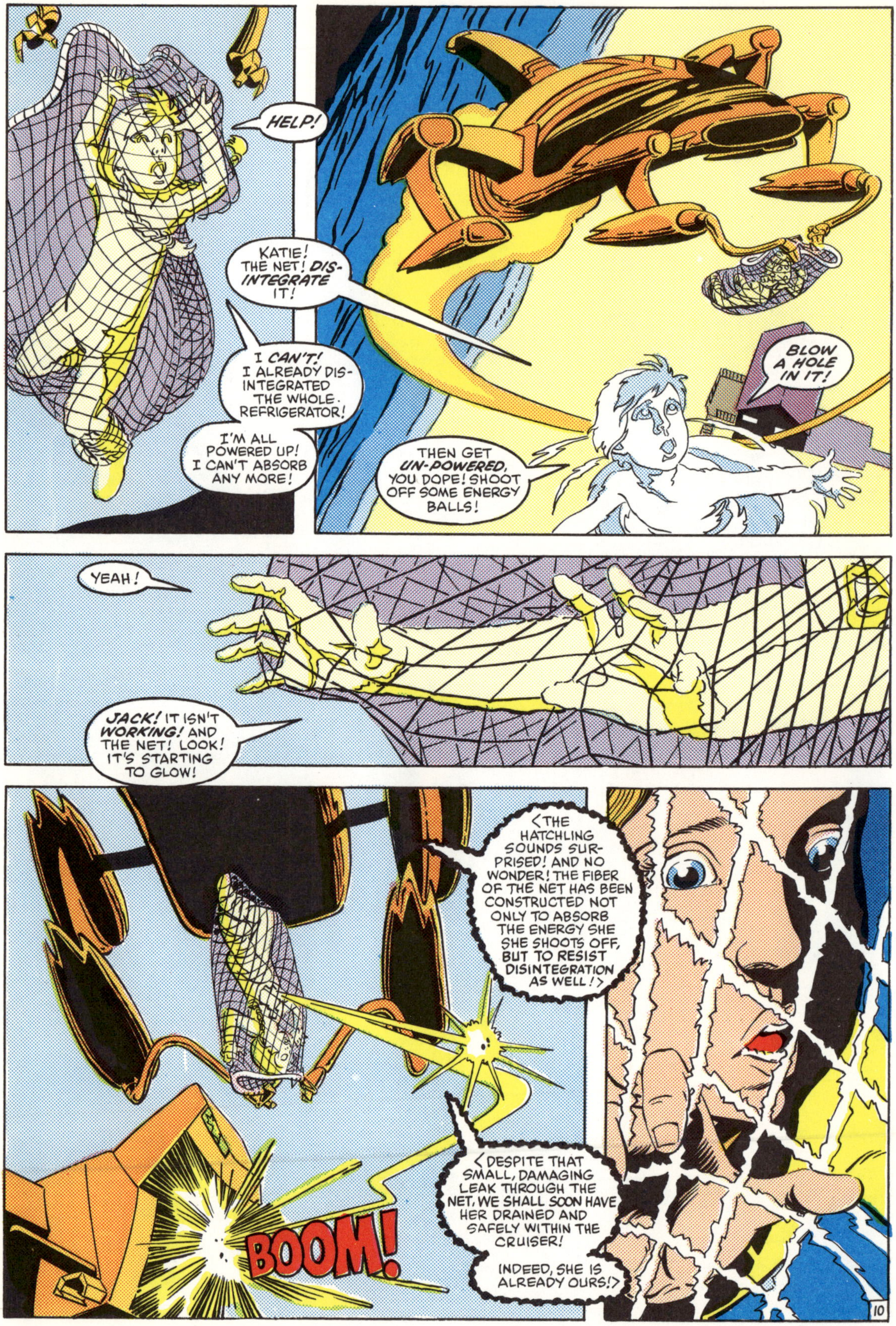
HELP!
KATIE! THE NET! DIS-INTEGRATE IT!
I CAN'T! I ALREADY DIS-INTEGRATED THE WHOLE REFRIGERATOR!
I'M ALL POWERED UP! I CAN'T ABSORB ANY MORE!
BLOW A HOLE IN IT!
THEN GET UN-POWERED, YOU DOPE! SHOOT OFF SOME ENERGY BALLS!
YEAH!
JACK! IT ISN'T WORKING! AND THE NET! LOOK! IT'S STARTING TO GLOW!
<THE HATCHLING SOUNDS SUR-PRISED! AND NO WONDER! THE FIBER OF THE NET HAS BEEN CONSTRUCTED NOT ONLY TO ABSORB THE ENERGY SHE SHE SHOOTS OFF, BUT TO RESIST DISINTEGRATION AS WELL!>
BOOM!
<DESPITE THAT SMALL, DAMAGING LEAK THROUGH THE NET, WE SHALL SOON HAVE HER DRAINED AND SAFELY WITHIN THE CRUISER!
INDEED, SHE IS ALREADY OURS!>
10

MEANWHILE...
GREAT! KATIE'S ENERGY BALLS MADE THE SNARKS DUCK OUT OF THE WAY! SHE ACTUALLY CLEARED THE PATH FOR ME...
...THOUGH HOW SHE MANAGED TO AIM THROUGH OLD MASS-MASTER I'LL NEVER KNOW! HIS COVER'S SO THICK I CAN'T SEE HER FROM UP HERE!
<THE FLYING ONE! AFTER HER!>
<SHE'S HEADING INTO OUR LAUNCH BAY! IS SHE INSANE?>
MOM AND DAD ARE IN HERE--ON AN UPPER LEVEL SOMEWHERE! IF ONLY I--
JULIE!
CAREFUL! THE AIRLOCK! IT'S SHUT--
FRIDAY...? NO WONDER WE COULDN'T FIND YOU!
UNF!
THUKGGG!
MINUTES LATER...
<THESE THREE, AT LEAST, ARE OURS! SMALL, NEAT BUNDLES OF INCREDIBLE POTENTIAL FOR DESTRUCTION!>
<THE ANESTHETIC PROPERTIES OF THE NEURO-FIBERS WILL KEEP THEM QUIESCENT--AS IT DOES THEIR PARENTS--UNTIL OUR ARRIVAL ON THE MOTHERSHIP!>
<EVEN SO, THEY, LIKE THEIR PARENTS, ARE TO REMAIN UNDER GUARD AND UNDER NO CIRCUMSTANCES MUST THE NEURO-FIBER BE REMOVED!>
<YOUR PARDON, CAPTAIN! THE QUEEN MOTHER WISHES TO SPEAK WITH YOU ON THE SCREEN!>

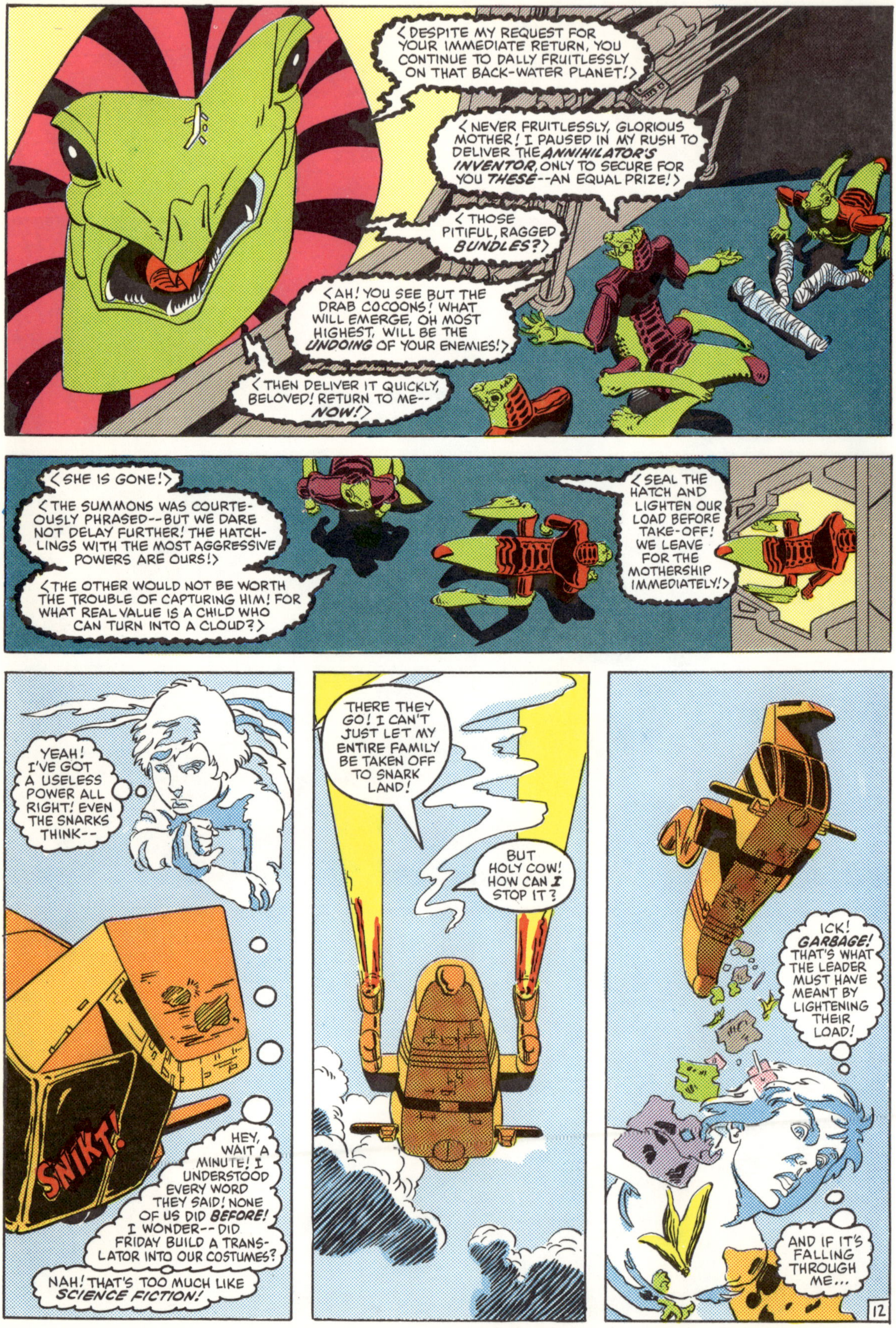

<DESPITE MY REQUEST FOR YOUR IMMEDIATE RETURN, YOU CONTINUE TO DALLY FRUITLESSLY ON THAT BACK-WATER PLANET!>
<NEVER FRUITLESSLY, GLORIOUS MOTHER! I PAUSED IN MY RUSH TO DELIVER THE ANNIHILATOR'S INVENTOR, ONLY TO SECURE FOR YOU THESE--AN EQUAL PRIZE!>
<THOSE PITIFUL, RAGGED BUNDLES?>
<AH! YOU SEE BUT THE DRAB COCOONS! WHAT WILL EMERGE, OH MOST HIGHEST, WILL BE THE UNDOING OF YOUR ENEMIES!>
<THEN DELIVER IT QUICKLY, BELOVED! RETURN TO ME--NOW!>
<SHE IS GONE!>
<THE SUMMONS WAS COURTEOUSLY PHRASED--BUT WE DARE NOT DELAY FURTHER! THE HATCHLINGS WITH THE MOST AGGRESSIVE POWERS ARE OURS!>
<THE OTHER WOULD NOT BE WORTH THE TROUBLE OF CAPTURING HIM! FOR WHAT REAL VALUE IS A CHILD WHO CAN TURN INTO A CLOUD?>
<SEAL THE HATCH AND LIGHTEN OUR LOAD BEFORE TAKE-OFF! WE LEAVE FOR THE MOTHERSHIP IMMEDIATELY!>
YEAH! I'VE GOT A USELESS POWER ALL RIGHT! EVEN THE SNARKS THINK--
SNIKT!
HEY, WAIT A MINUTE! I UNDERSTOOD EVERY WORD THEY SAID! NONE OF US DID BEFORE! I WONDER--DID FRIDAY BUILD A TRANSLATOR INTO OUR COSTUMES?
NAH! THAT'S TOO MUCH LIKE SCIENCE FICTION!
THERE THEY GO! I CAN'T JUST LET MY ENTIRE FAMILY BE TAKEN OFF TO SNARK LAND!
BUT HOLY COW! HOW CAN I STOP IT?
ICK! GARBAGE! THAT'S WHAT THE LEADER MUST HAVE MEANT BY LIGHTENING THEIR LOAD!
AND IF IT'S FALLING THROUGH ME...

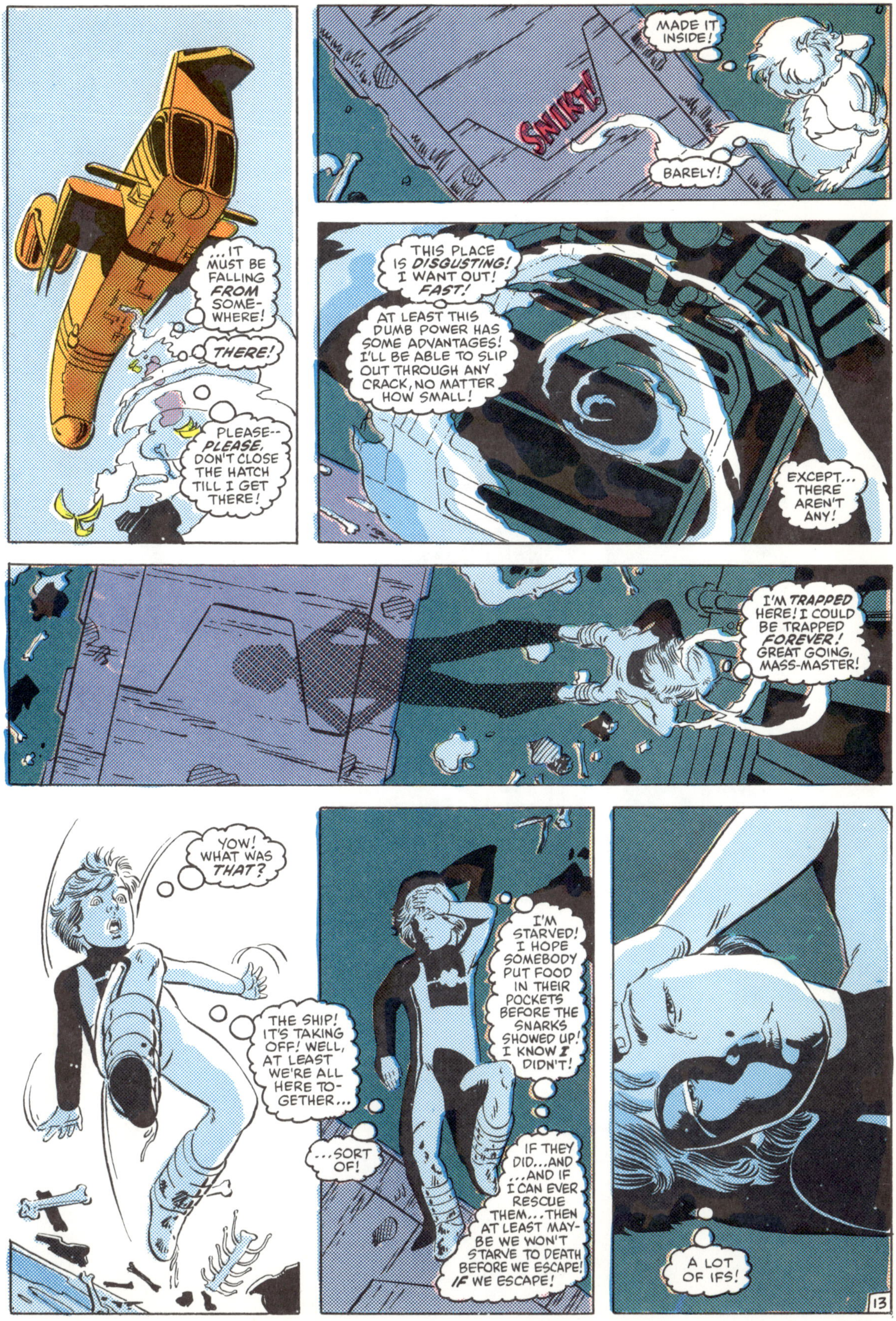
...IT MUST BE FALLING FROM SOME-WHERE!
THERE!
PLEASE-- PLEASE, DON'T CLOSE THE HATCH TILL I GET THERE!
MADE IT INSIDE!
SNIKT!
BARELY!
THIS PLACE IS DISGUSTING! I WANT OUT! FAST!
AT LEAST THIS DUMB POWER HAS SOME ADVANTAGES! I'LL BE ABLE TO SLIP OUT THROUGH ANY CRACK, NO MATTER HOW SMALL!
EXCEPT... THERE AREN'T ANY!
I'M TRAPPED HERE! I COULD BE TRAPPED FOREVER! GREAT GOING, MASS-MASTER!
YOW! WHAT WAS THAT?
THE SHIP! IT'S TAKING OFF! WELL, AT LEAST WE'RE ALL HERE TO-GETHER...
...SORT OF!
I'M STARVED! I HOPE SOMEBODY PUT FOOD IN THEIR POCKETS BEFORE THE SNARKS SHOWED UP! I KNOW I DIDN'T!
IF THEY DID... AND ...AND IF I CAN EVER RESCUE THEM... THEN AT LEAST MAY-BE WE WON'T STARVE TO DEATH BEFORE WE ESCAPE! IF WE ESCAPE!
A LOT OF IFS!

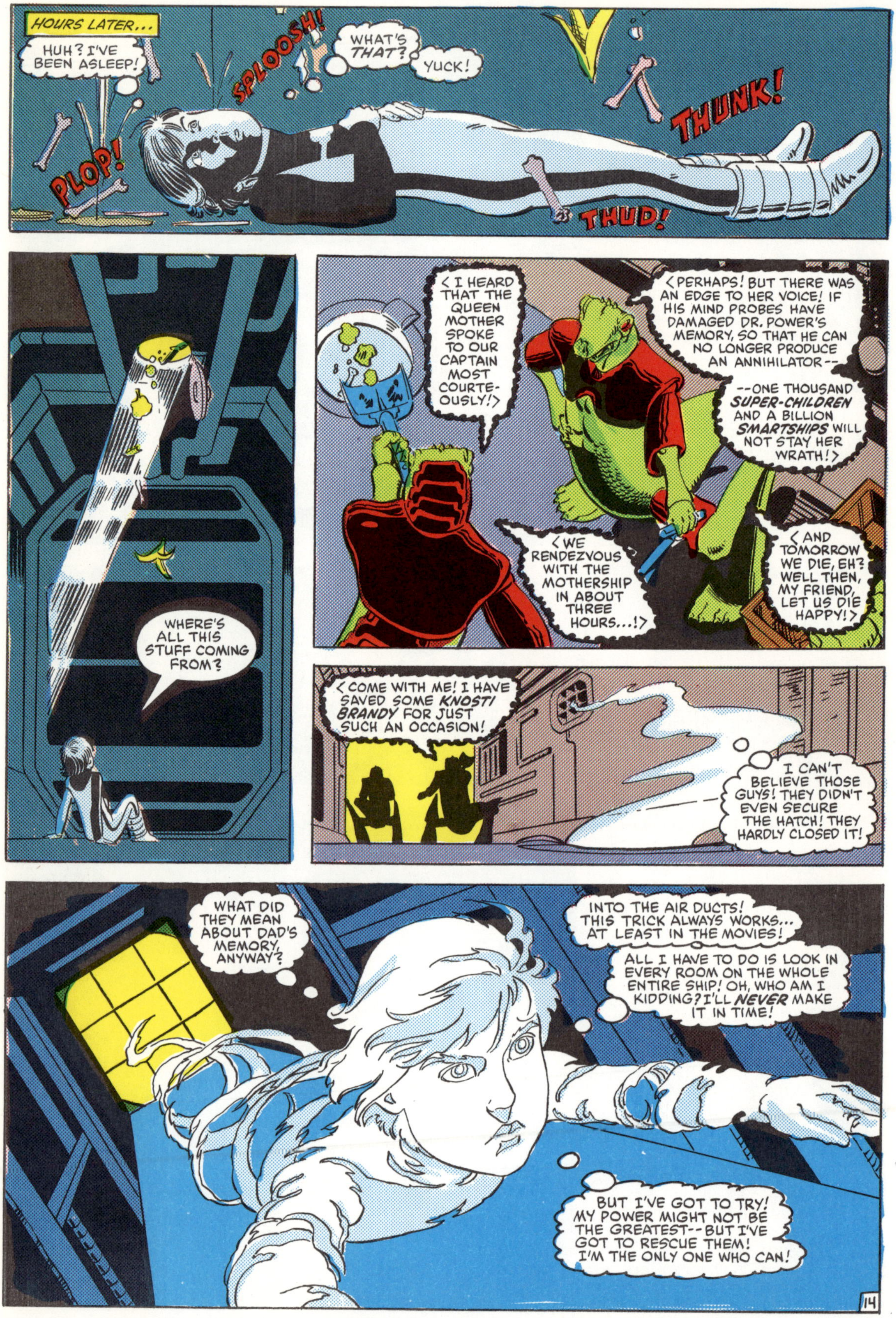
HOURS LATER...
HUH? I'VE BEEN ASLEEP!
SPLOOSH!
WHAT'S *THAT*?
YUCK!
PLOP!
THUNK!
THUD!
WHERE'S ALL THIS STUFF COMING FROM?
< I HEARD THAT THE QUEEN MOTHER SPOKE TO OUR CAPTAIN MOST COURTE-OUSLY! >
< PERHAPS! BUT THERE WAS AN EDGE TO HER VOICE! IF HIS MIND PROBES HAVE DAMAGED DR. POWER'S MEMORY, SO THAT HE CAN NO LONGER PRODUCE AN ANNIHILATOR--
--ONE THOUSAND ***SUPER-CHILDREN*** AND A BILLION ***SMARTSHIPS*** WILL NOT STAY HER WRATH! >
< WE RENDEZVOUS WITH THE MOTHERSHIP IN ABOUT THREE HOURS...! >
< AND TOMORROW WE DIE, EH? WELL THEN, MY FRIEND, LET US DIE HAPPY! >
< COME WITH ME! I HAVE SAVED SOME ***KNOSTI BRANDY*** FOR JUST SUCH AN OCCASION! >
I CAN'T BELIEVE THOSE GUYS! THEY DIDN'T EVEN SECURE THE HATCH! THEY HARDLY CLOSED IT!
WHAT DID THEY MEAN ABOUT DAD'S MEMORY, ANYWAY?
INTO THE AIR DUCTS! THIS TRICK ALWAYS WORKS... AT LEAST IN THE MOVIES!
ALL I HAVE TO DO IS LOOK IN EVERY ROOM ON THE WHOLE ENTIRE SHIP! OH, WHO AM I KIDDING? I'LL ***NEVER*** MAKE IT IN TIME!
BUT I'VE GOT TO TRY! MY POWER MIGHT NOT BE THE GREATEST--BUT I'VE GOT TO RESCUE THEM! I'M THE ONLY ONE WHO CAN!
14

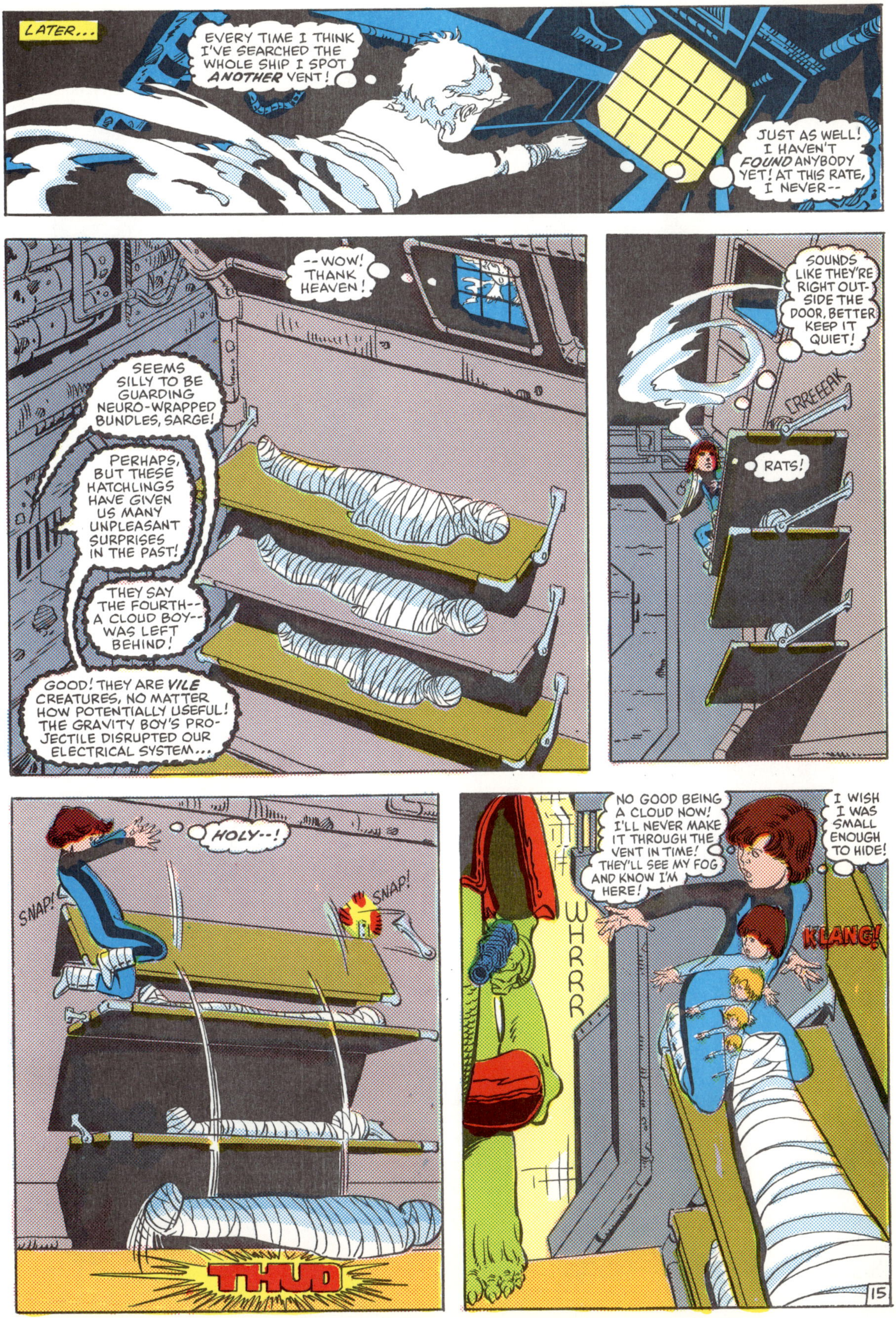
LATER...
EVERY TIME I THINK I'VE SEARCHED THE WHOLE SHIP I SPOT ANOTHER VENT!
JUST AS WELL! I HAVEN'T FOUND ANYBODY YET! AT THIS RATE, I NEVER--
--WOW! THANK HEAVEN!
SEEMS SILLY TO BE GUARDING NEURO-WRAPPED BUNDLES, SARGE!
PERHAPS, BUT THESE HATCHLINGS HAVE GIVEN US MANY UNPLEASANT SURPRISES IN THE PAST!
THEY SAY THE FOURTH-- A CLOUD BOY-- WAS LEFT BEHIND!
GOOD! THEY ARE VILE CREATURES, NO MATTER HOW POTENTIALLY USEFUL! THE GRAVITY BOY'S PROJECTILE DISRUPTED OUR ELECTRICAL SYSTEM...
SOUNDS LIKE THEY'RE RIGHT OUTSIDE THE DOOR. BETTER KEEP IT QUIET!
CRREEEAK
RATS!
HOLY--!
SNAP!
SNAP!
THUD
NO GOOD BEING A CLOUD NOW! I'LL NEVER MAKE IT THROUGH THE VENT IN TIME! THEY'LL SEE MY FOG AND KNOW I'M HERE!
I WISH I WAS SMALL ENOUGH TO HIDE!
WHRRR
KLANG!
15

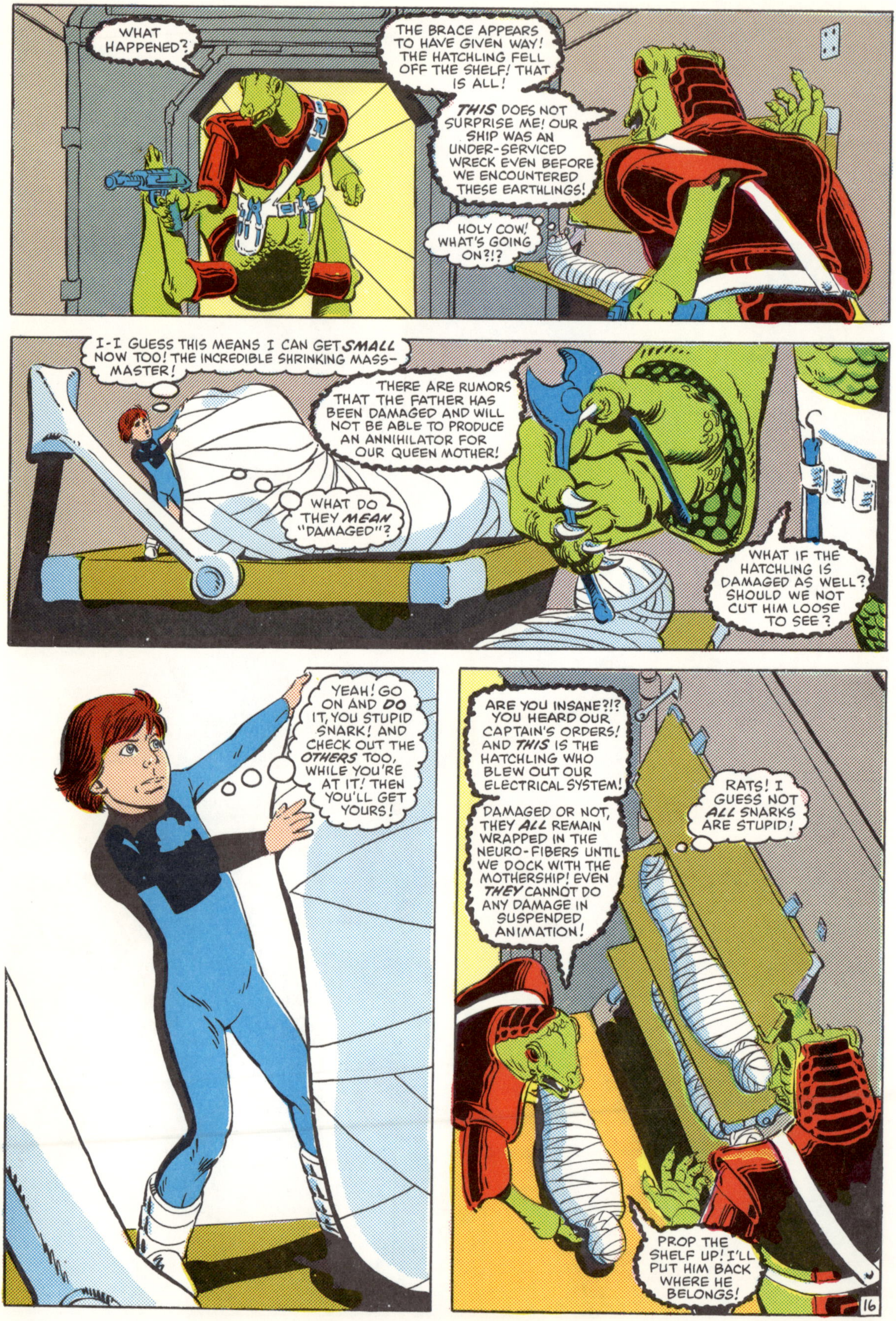
WHAT HAPPENED?
THE BRACE APPEARS TO HAVE GIVEN WAY! THE HATCHLING FELL OFF THE SHELF! THAT IS ALL!
THIS DOES NOT SURPRISE ME! OUR SHIP WAS AN UNDER-SERVICED WRECK EVEN BEFORE WE ENCOUNTERED THESE EARTHLINGS!
HOLY COW! WHAT'S GOING ON?!?
I-I GUESS THIS MEANS I CAN GET SMALL NOW TOO! THE INCREDIBLE SHRINKING MASS-MASTER!
THERE ARE RUMORS THAT THE FATHER HAS BEEN DAMAGED AND WILL NOT BE ABLE TO PRODUCE AN ANNIHILATOR FOR OUR QUEEN MOTHER!
WHAT DO THEY MEAN "DAMAGED"?
WHAT IF THE HATCHLING IS DAMAGED AS WELL? SHOULD WE NOT CUT HIM LOOSE TO SEE?
YEAH! GO ON AND DO IT, YOU STUPID SNARK! AND CHECK OUT THE OTHERS TOO, WHILE YOU'RE AT IT! THEN YOU'LL GET YOURS!
ARE YOU INSANE?!? YOU HEARD OUR CAPTAIN'S ORDERS! AND THIS IS THE HATCHLING WHO BLEW OUT OUR ELECTRICAL SYSTEM!
DAMAGED OR NOT, THEY ALL REMAIN WRAPPED IN THE NEURO-FIBERS UNTIL WE DOCK WITH THE MOTHERSHIP! EVEN THEY CANNOT DO ANY DAMAGE IN SUSPENDED ANIMATION!
RATS! I GUESS NOT ALL SNARKS ARE STUPID!
PROP THE SHELF UP! I'LL PUT HIM BACK WHERE HE BELONGS!
16

SNAP!
OH NO! NOT AGAIN!
SNAP!
KLANG!
WHA--?
WHY DO THE SHELVES KEEP DOING THAT?
THUMP!
OOF!
WOW!
THUD!
I MUST BE SUPER-STRONG WHEN I'M SUPER-SMALL!
ALL RIGHT, MONSTER! IT'S YOU AGAINST MASS-MASTER! SURRENDER OR--

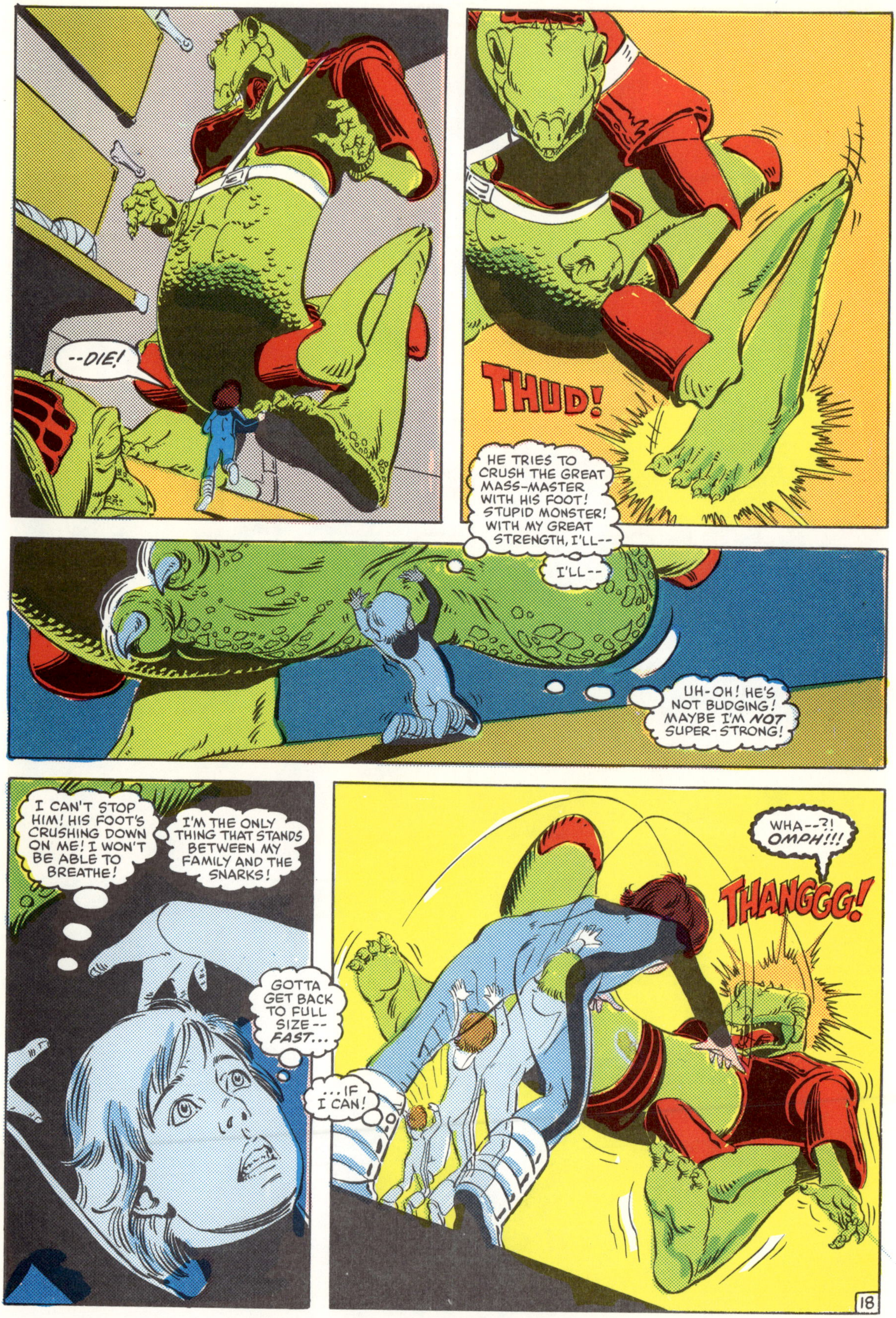

--DIE!
THUD!
HE TRIES TO CRUSH THE GREAT MASS-MASTER WITH HIS FOOT! STUPID MONSTER! WITH MY GREAT STRENGTH, I'LL--
I'LL--
UH-OH! HE'S NOT BUDGING! MAYBE I'M NOT SUPER-STRONG!
I CAN'T STOP HIM! HIS FOOT'S CRUSHING DOWN ON ME! I WON'T BE ABLE TO BREATHE!
I'M THE ONLY THING THAT STANDS BETWEEN MY FAMILY AND THE SNARKS!
GOTTA GET BACK TO FULL SIZE-- FAST...
...IF I CAN!
WHA--?! OMPH!!!
THANGGG!

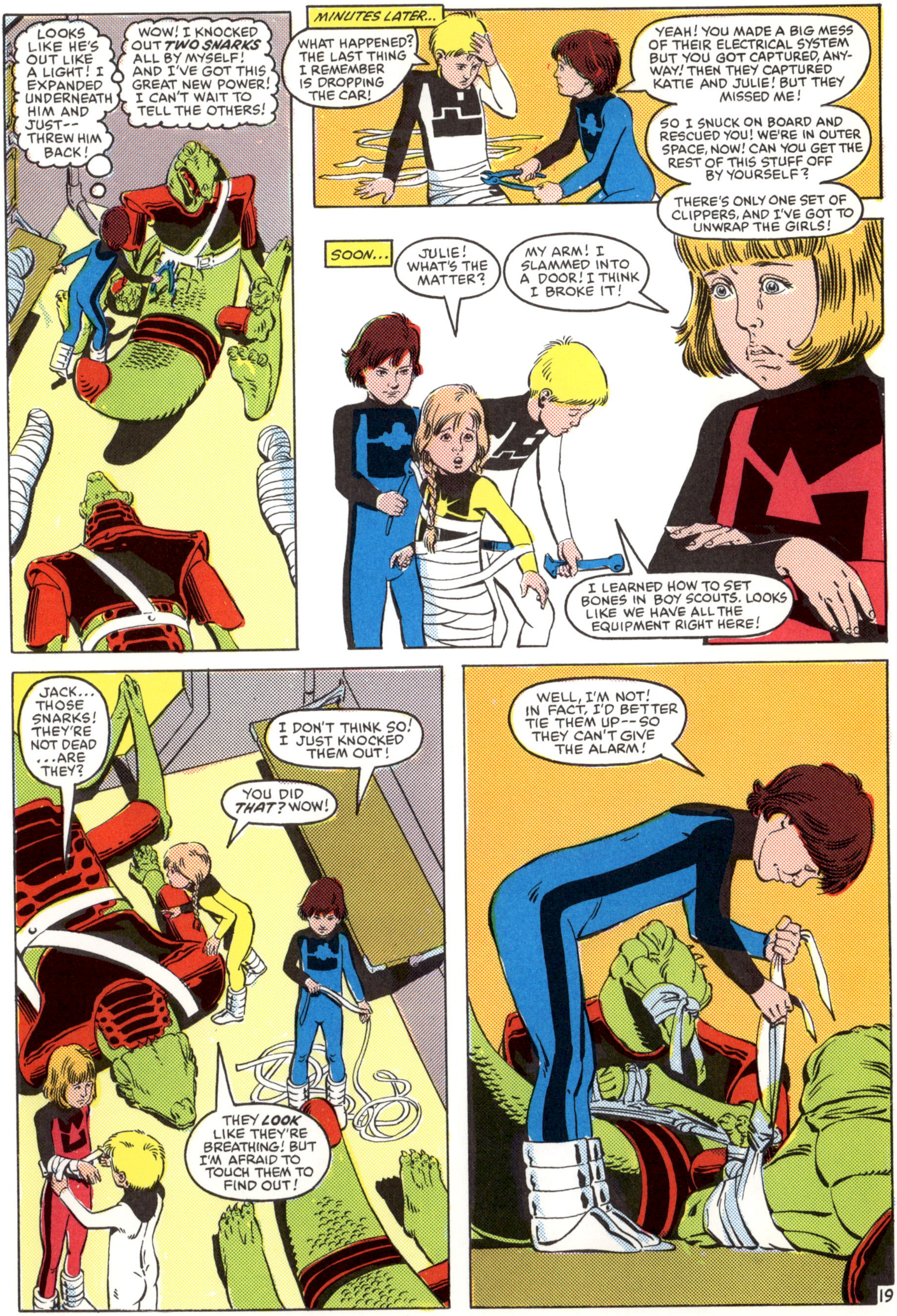
LOOKS LIKE HE'S OUT LIKE A LIGHT! I EXPANDED UNDERNEATH HIM AND JUST-- THREW HIM BACK!
WOW! I KNOCKED OUT TWO SNARKS ALL BY MYSELF! AND I'VE GOT THIS GREAT NEW POWER! I CAN'T WAIT TO TELL THE OTHERS!
MINUTES LATER...
WHAT HAPPENED? THE LAST THING I REMEMBER IS DROPPING THE CAR!
YEAH! YOU MADE A BIG MESS OF THEIR ELECTRICAL SYSTEM BUT YOU GOT CAPTURED, ANY-WAY! THEN THEY CAPTURED KATIE AND JULIE! BUT THEY MISSED ME!
SO I SNUCK ON BOARD AND RESCUED YOU! WE'RE IN OUTER SPACE, NOW! CAN YOU GET THE REST OF THIS STUFF OFF BY YOURSELF?
THERE'S ONLY ONE SET OF CLIPPERS, AND I'VE GOT TO UNWRAP THE GIRLS!
SOON...
JULIE! WHAT'S THE MATTER?
MY ARM! I SLAMMED INTO A DOOR! I THINK I BROKE IT!
I LEARNED HOW TO SET BONES IN BOY SCOUTS. LOOKS LIKE WE HAVE ALL THE EQUIPMENT RIGHT HERE!
JACK... THOSE SNARKS! THEY'RE NOT DEAD ...ARE THEY?
I DON'T THINK SO! I JUST KNOCKED THEM OUT!
YOU DID THAT? WOW!
THEY LOOK LIKE THEY'RE BREATHING! BUT I'M AFRAID TO TOUCH THEM TO FIND OUT!
WELL, I'M NOT! IN FACT, I'D BETTER TIE THEM UP--SO THEY CAN'T GIVE THE ALARM!

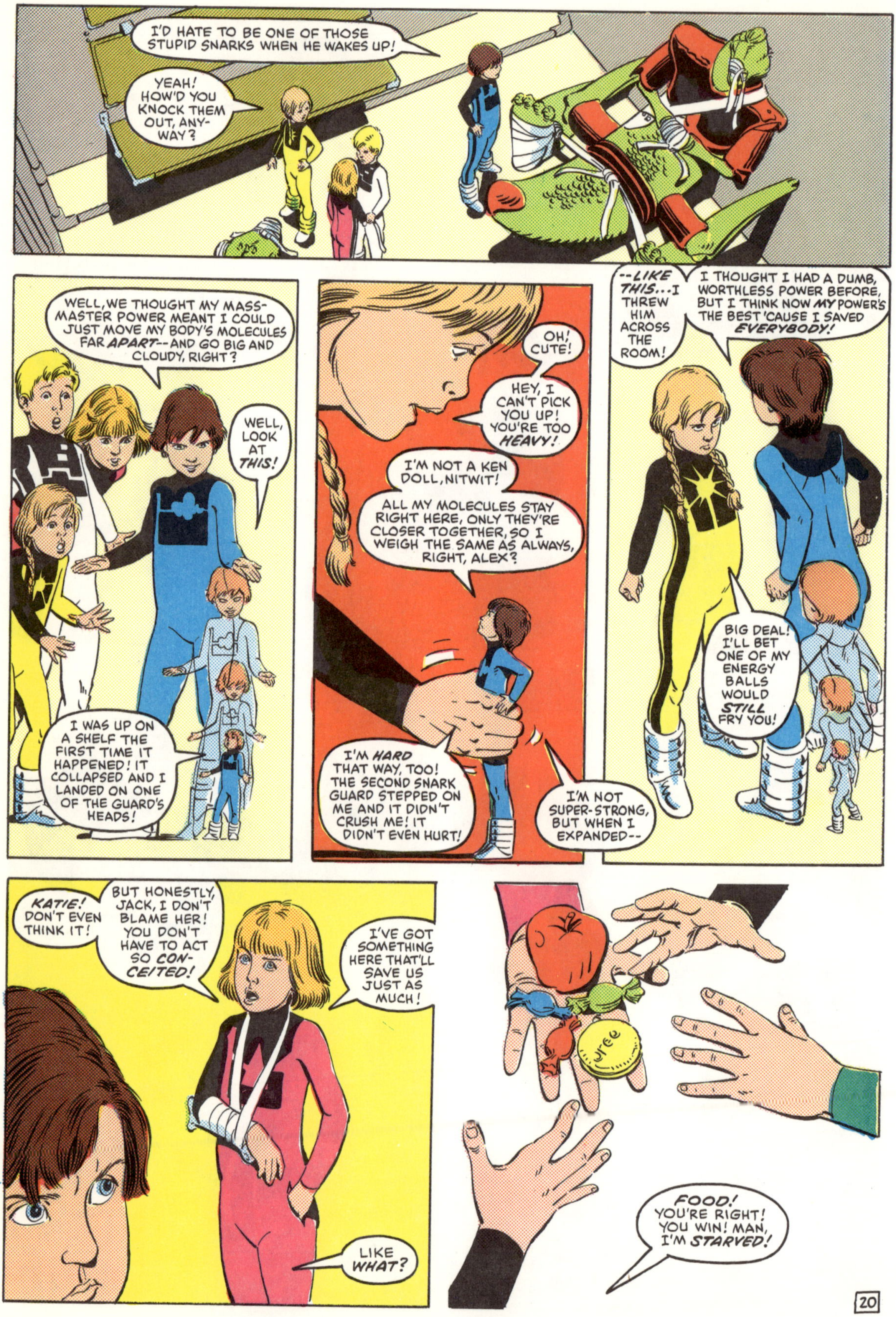
I'D HATE TO BE ONE OF THOSE STUPID SNARKS WHEN HE WAKES UP!
YEAH! HOW'D YOU KNOCK THEM OUT, ANYWAY?
WELL, WE THOUGHT MY MASS-MASTER POWER MEANT I COULD JUST MOVE MY BODY'S MOLECULES FAR APART--AND GO BIG AND CLOUDY, RIGHT?
WELL, LOOK AT THIS!
I WAS UP ON A SHELF THE FIRST TIME IT HAPPENED! IT COLLAPSED AND I LANDED ON ONE OF THE GUARD'S HEADS!
OH! CUTE!
HEY, I CAN'T PICK YOU UP! YOU'RE TOO HEAVY!
I'M NOT A KEN DOLL, NITWIT!
ALL MY MOLECULES STAY RIGHT HERE, ONLY THEY'RE CLOSER TOGETHER, SO I WEIGH THE SAME AS ALWAYS, RIGHT, ALEX?
I'M HARD THAT WAY, TOO! THE SECOND SNARK GUARD STEPPED ON ME AND IT DIDN'T CRUSH ME! IT DIDN'T EVEN HURT!
I'M NOT SUPER-STRONG, BUT WHEN I EXPANDED--
--LIKE THIS...I THREW HIM ACROSS THE ROOM!
I THOUGHT I HAD A DUMB, WORTHLESS POWER BEFORE, BUT I THINK NOW MY POWER'S THE BEST 'CAUSE I SAVED EVERYBODY!
BIG DEAL! I'LL BET ONE OF MY ENERGY BALLS WOULD STILL FRY YOU!
KATIE! DON'T EVEN THINK IT!
BUT HONESTLY, JACK, I DON'T BLAME HER! YOU DON'T HAVE TO ACT SO CON-CEITED!
I'VE GOT SOMETHING HERE THAT'LL SAVE US JUST AS MUCH!
LIKE WHAT?
FOOD! YOU'RE RIGHT! YOU WIN! MAN, I'M STARVED!

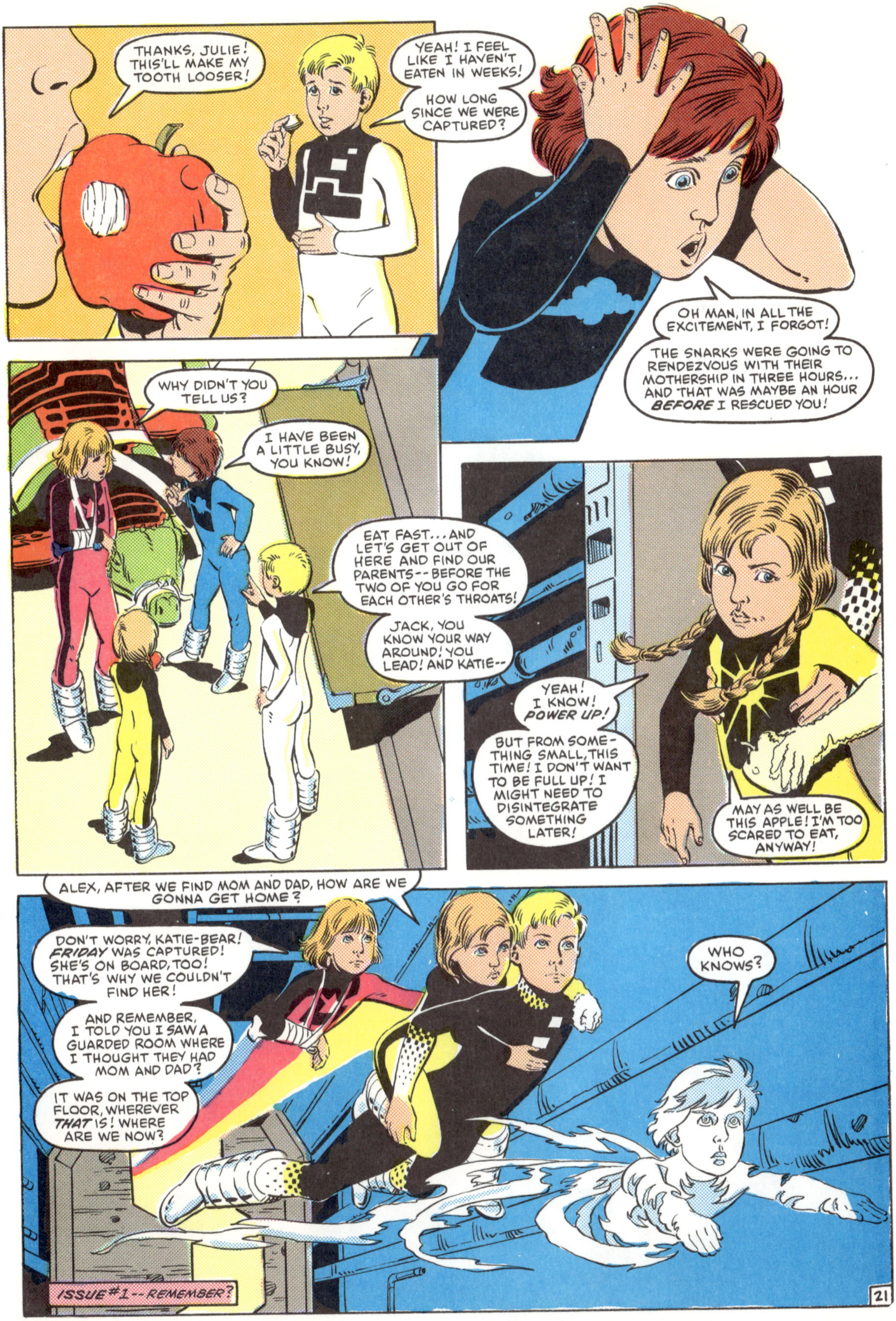
THANKS, JULIE! THIS'LL MAKE MY TOOTH LOOSER!
YEAH! I FEEL LIKE I HAVEN'T EATEN IN WEEKS!
HOW LONG SINCE WE WERE CAPTURED?
OH MAN, IN ALL THE EXCITEMENT, I FORGOT!
THE SNARKS WERE GOING TO RENDEZVOUS WITH THEIR MOTHERSHIP IN THREE HOURS... AND THAT WAS MAYBE AN HOUR ***BEFORE*** I RESCUED YOU!
WHY DIDN'T YOU TELL US?
I HAVE BEEN A LITTLE BUSY, YOU KNOW!
EAT FAST... AND LET'S GET OUT OF HERE AND FIND OUR PARENTS--BEFORE THE TWO OF YOU GO FOR EACH OTHER'S THROATS!
JACK, YOU KNOW YOUR WAY AROUND! YOU LEAD! AND KATIE--
YEAH! I KNOW! ***POWER UP!***
BUT FROM SOMETHING SMALL, THIS TIME! I DON'T WANT TO BE FULL UP! I MIGHT NEED TO DISINTEGRATE SOMETHING LATER!
MAY AS WELL BE THIS APPLE! I'M TOO SCARED TO EAT, ANYWAY!
ALEX, AFTER WE FIND MOM AND DAD, HOW ARE WE GONNA GET HOME?
DON'T WORRY, KATIE-BEAR! ***FRIDAY*** WAS CAPTURED! SHE'S ON BOARD, TOO! THAT'S WHY WE COULDN'T FIND HER!
AND REMEMBER, I TOLD YOU I ***SAW*** A GUARDED ROOM WHERE I THOUGHT THEY HAD MOM AND DAD?
IT WAS ON THE TOP FLOOR, WHEREVER ***THAT*** IS! WHERE ARE WE NOW?
WHO KNOWS?
ISSUE #1--REMEMBER?
21

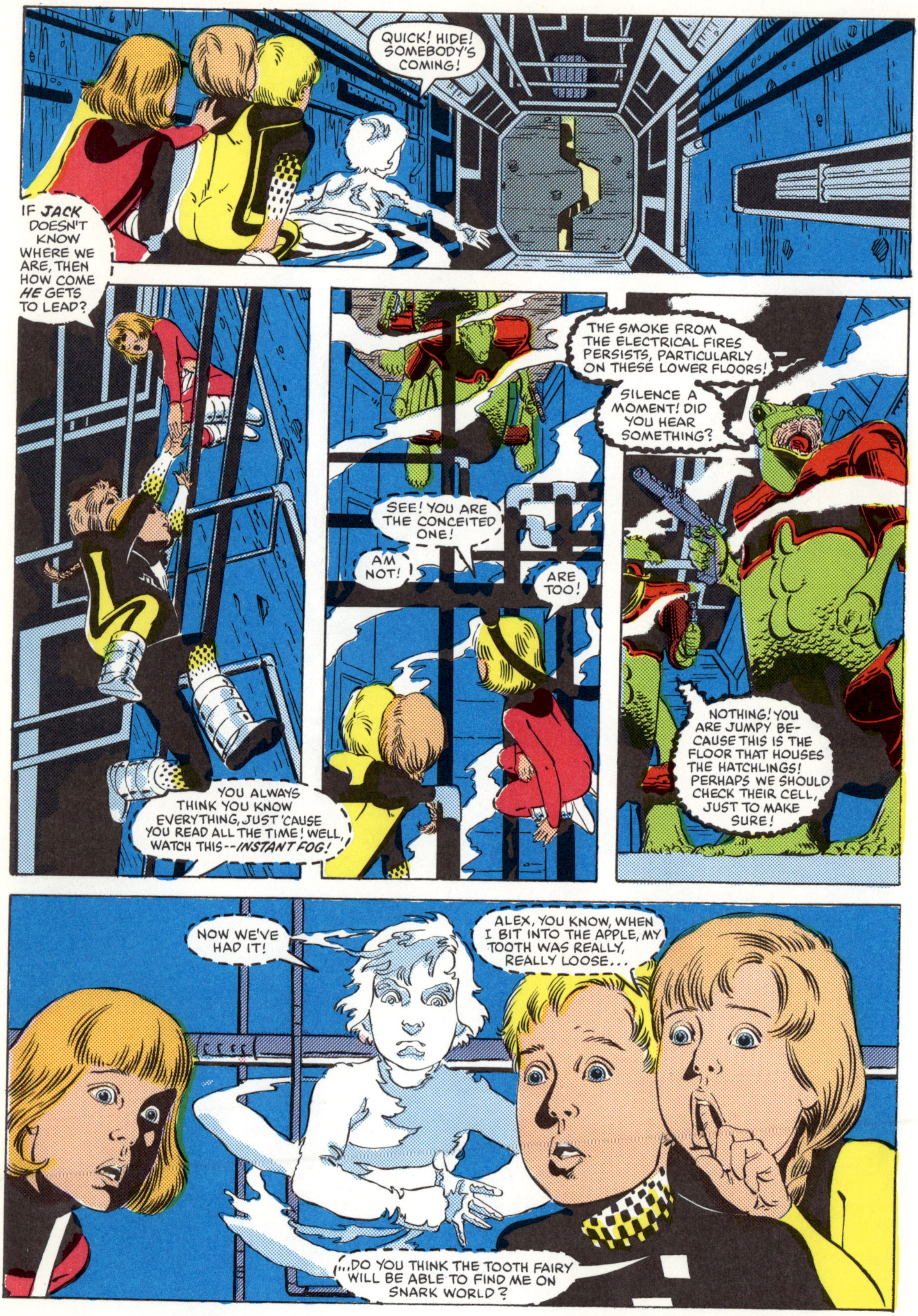

QUICK! HIDE! SOMEBODY'S COMING!
IF JACK DOESN'T KNOW WHERE WE ARE, THEN HOW COME HE GETS TO LEAD?
YOU ALWAYS THINK YOU KNOW EVERYTHING, JUST 'CAUSE YOU READ ALL THE TIME! WELL, WATCH THIS--INSTANT FOG!
SEE! YOU ARE THE CONCEITED ONE!
AM NOT!
ARE TOO!
THE SMOKE FROM THE ELECTRICAL FIRES PERSISTS, PARTICULARLY ON THESE LOWER FLOORS!
SILENCE A MOMENT! DID YOU HEAR SOMETHING?
NOTHING! YOU ARE JUMPY BE-CAUSE THIS IS THE FLOOR THAT HOUSES THE HATCHLINGS! PERHAPS WE SHOULD CHECK THEIR CELL, JUST TO MAKE SURE!
NOW WE'VE HAD IT!
ALEX, YOU KNOW, WHEN I BIT INTO THE APPLE, MY TOOTH WAS REALLY, REALLY LOOSE...
...DO YOU THINK THE TOOTH FAIRY WILL BE ABLE TO FIND ME ON SNARK WORLD?

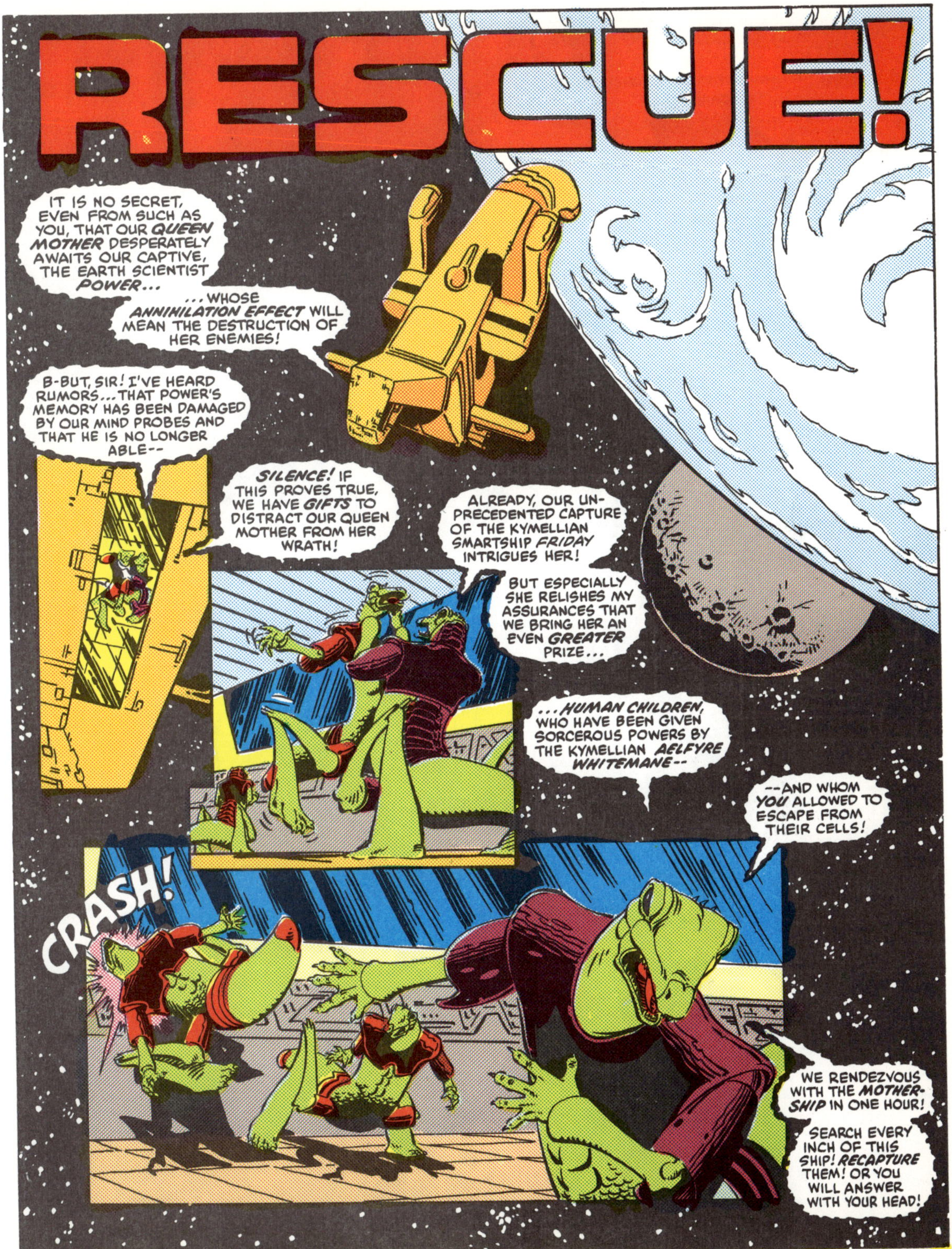

LOUISE SIMONSON WRITER | JUNE BRIGMAN PENCILER | BOB WIACEK INKER | JOE ROSEN LETTERER | GLYNIS WEIN COLORIST | CARL POTTS EDITOR | JIM SHOOTER EDITOR-IN-CHIEF

SOON...
CAREFUL! THOSE HATCHLINGS COULD BE ANYWHERE!
THE ELECTRICAL FIRES CAUSED BY THEIR ATTACK ON OUR BRIDGE* HAVE CREATED A SMOKY HAZE THAT PERMEATES THIS CORRIDOR!
*LAST ISSUE.
ODD, THOUGH, HOW IT DOESN'T REEK LIKE--
CREAK!
QUIET, KATIE!
MY CLOUD-FORM CAN HIDE US, BUT IT DOESN'T MUFFLE SOUND!
AND STOP SQUIRMING! YOU'RE WEIGHTLESS AND FLOATING ONLY 'CAUSE I'M HOLDING YOU!
JACK, I DIDN'T CREAK! AND I'M NOT SQUIRMING, ALEX! I'M WIGGLING MY LOOSE TOOTH!
CREAK!
I- IT'S THIS PIPE! IT'S KIND OF WOBBLY... AND IT'S DRIPPING!
MAYBE I SHOULD FLY TO ANOTHER--
CRAK!
HELP!

JULIE!
SKA-KOW!

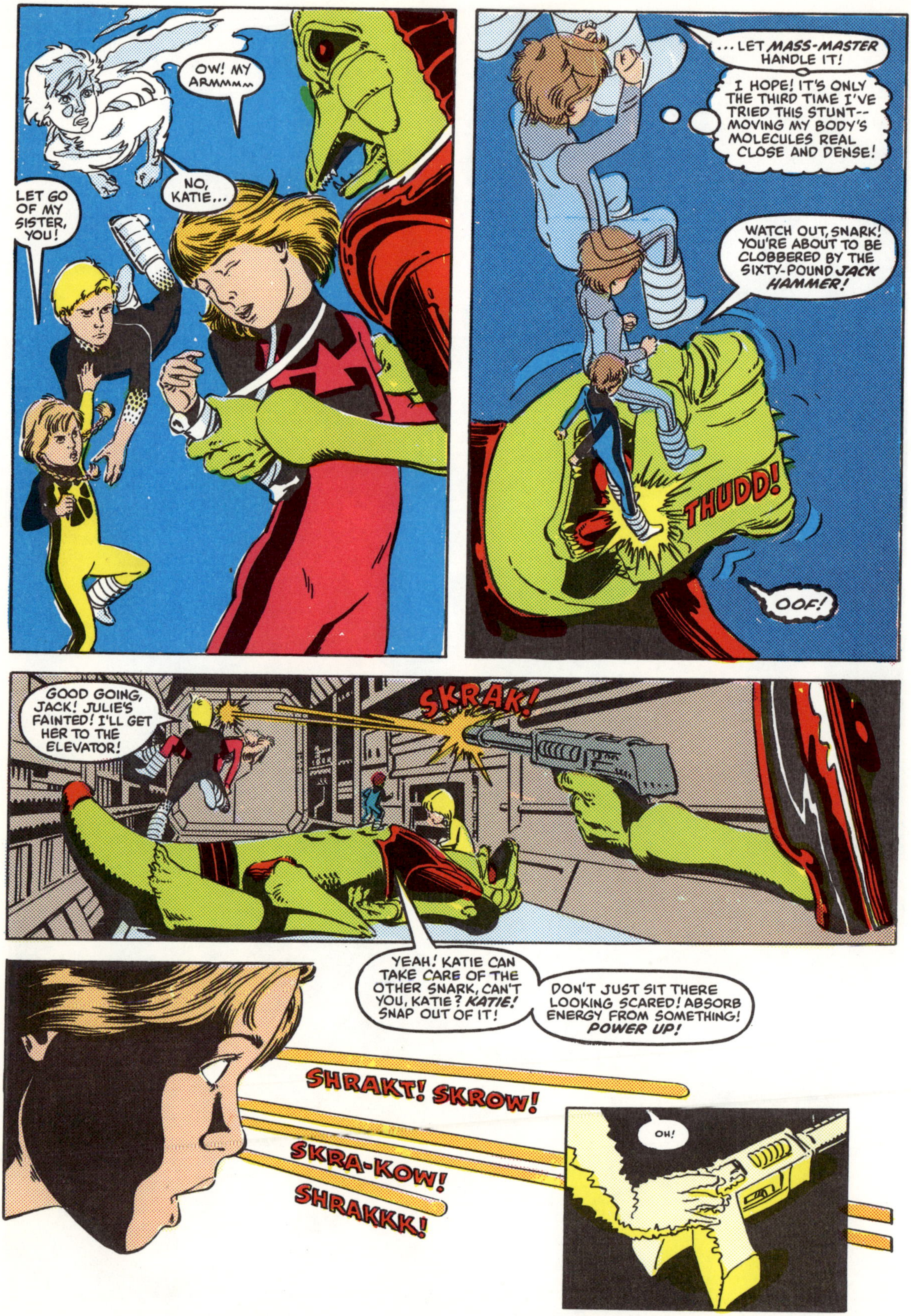
OW! MY ARMMMM
NO, KATIE...
LET GO OF MY SISTER, YOU!
...LET MASS-MASTER HANDLE IT!
I HOPE! IT'S ONLY THE THIRD TIME I'VE TRIED THIS STUNT-- MOVING MY BODY'S MOLECULES REAL CLOSE AND DENSE!
WATCH OUT, SNARK! YOU'RE ABOUT TO BE CLOBBERED BY THE SIXTY-POUND JACK HAMMER!
THUDD!
OOF!
GOOD GOING, JACK! JULIE'S FAINTED! I'LL GET HER TO THE ELEVATOR!
SKRAK!
YEAH! KATIE CAN TAKE CARE OF THE OTHER SNARK, CAN'T YOU, KATIE? KATIE! SNAP OUT OF IT!
DON'T JUST SIT THERE LOOKING SCARED! ABSORB ENERGY FROM SOMETHING! POWER UP!
SHRAKT! SKROW!
SKRA-KOW!
SHRAKKK!
OH!

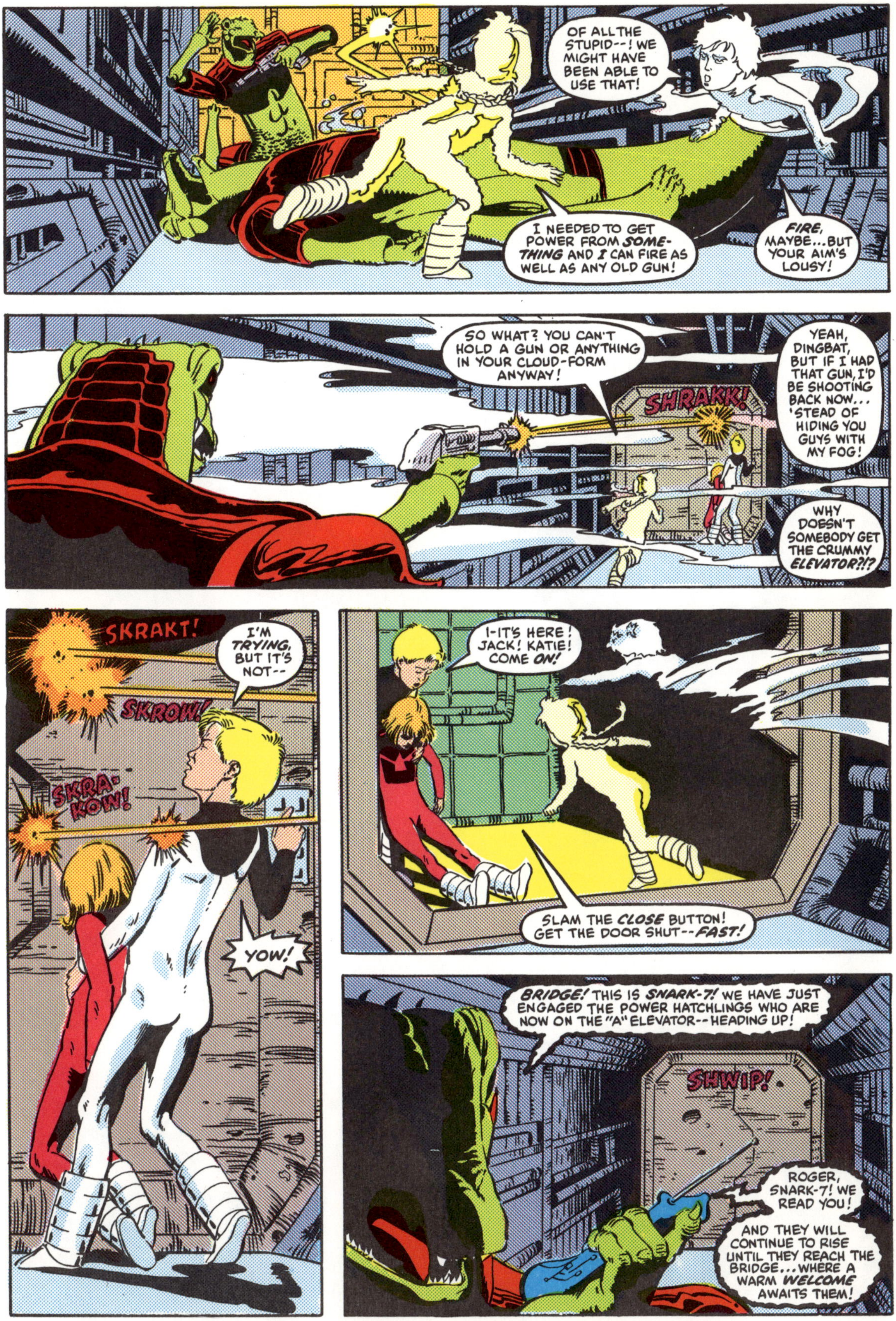

OF ALL THE STUPID--! WE MIGHT HAVE BEEN ABLE TO USE THAT!
I NEEDED TO GET POWER FROM SOMETHING AND I CAN FIRE AS WELL AS ANY OLD GUN!
FIRE, MAYBE... BUT YOUR AIM'S LOUSY!
SO WHAT? YOU CAN'T HOLD A GUN OR ANYTHING IN YOUR CLOUD-FORM ANYWAY!
SHRAKK!
YEAH, DINGBAT, BUT IF I HAD THAT GUN, I'D BE SHOOTING BACK NOW... 'STEAD OF HIDING YOU GUYS WITH MY FOG!
WHY DOESN'T SOMEBODY GET THE CRUMMY ELEVATOR?!?
SKRAKT!
I'M TRYING, BUT IT'S NOT--
SKROW!
SKRA-KOW!
YOW!
I-IT'S HERE! JACK! KATIE! COME ON!
SLAM THE CLOSE BUTTON! GET THE DOOR SHUT--FAST!
BRIDGE! THIS IS SNARK-7! WE HAVE JUST ENGAGED THE POWER HATCHLINGS WHO ARE NOW ON THE "A" ELEVATOR--HEADING UP!
SHWIP!
ROGER, SNARK-7! WE READ YOU!
AND THEY WILL CONTINUE TO RISE UNTIL THEY REACH THE BRIDGE... WHERE A WARM WELCOME AWAITS THEM!

MEANWHILE...
JULIE! JULIE! WAKE UP! ARE YOU OKAY?
Y-YEAH! WHERE ARE WE?
WE'RE ON THE ELEVATOR! ALEX SAID KEEP PRESSING THE TOP FLOOR...
...'CAUSE THAT'S WHERE YOU SAID MOM AND DAD PROBABLY ARE!
AT LEAST, THAT'S WHERE I SAW THE GUARDED ROOM THE FIRST TIME THE SNARKS CAPTURED US!
DOESN'T THIS ELEVATOR SEEM AWFULLY SLOW-MOVING, JACK?
YEAH! AT THIS RATE WE'LL STILL BE HERE WHEN THEY DOCK WITH THE MOTHERSHIP!
WE'LL NEVER RESCUE MOM AND DAD--OR FREE FRIDAY--AND WHITEY WILL HAVE GIVEN US HIS POWERS FOR NOTHING!
ALEX! YOU WERE HIT!
WOW! I'LL BET IT HURTS!
HEY--!
MY TOOTH!
I LOST MY TOOTH!
ALEX, CAN THE TOOTH FAIRY FIND ME HERE?
DON'T BE DUMB, KATIE! ONLY STUPID BABIES BELIEVE IN THE TOOTH FAIRY!
W-WHAT DO YOU MEAN?
JACK--!
HEY! WE'VE STOPPED!

FIRE!
UH OH!
NO!
CHINK!
SKRAKT!
MOVE!
SKROW!
SHRAKK!
RUN!
YOU GAVE IT YOUR BEST SHOT, KATIE! NOW DUCK!
THE POWER BALL!
IF IT STRIKES THE CONTROL BOARD--
BOOM!
YOW!

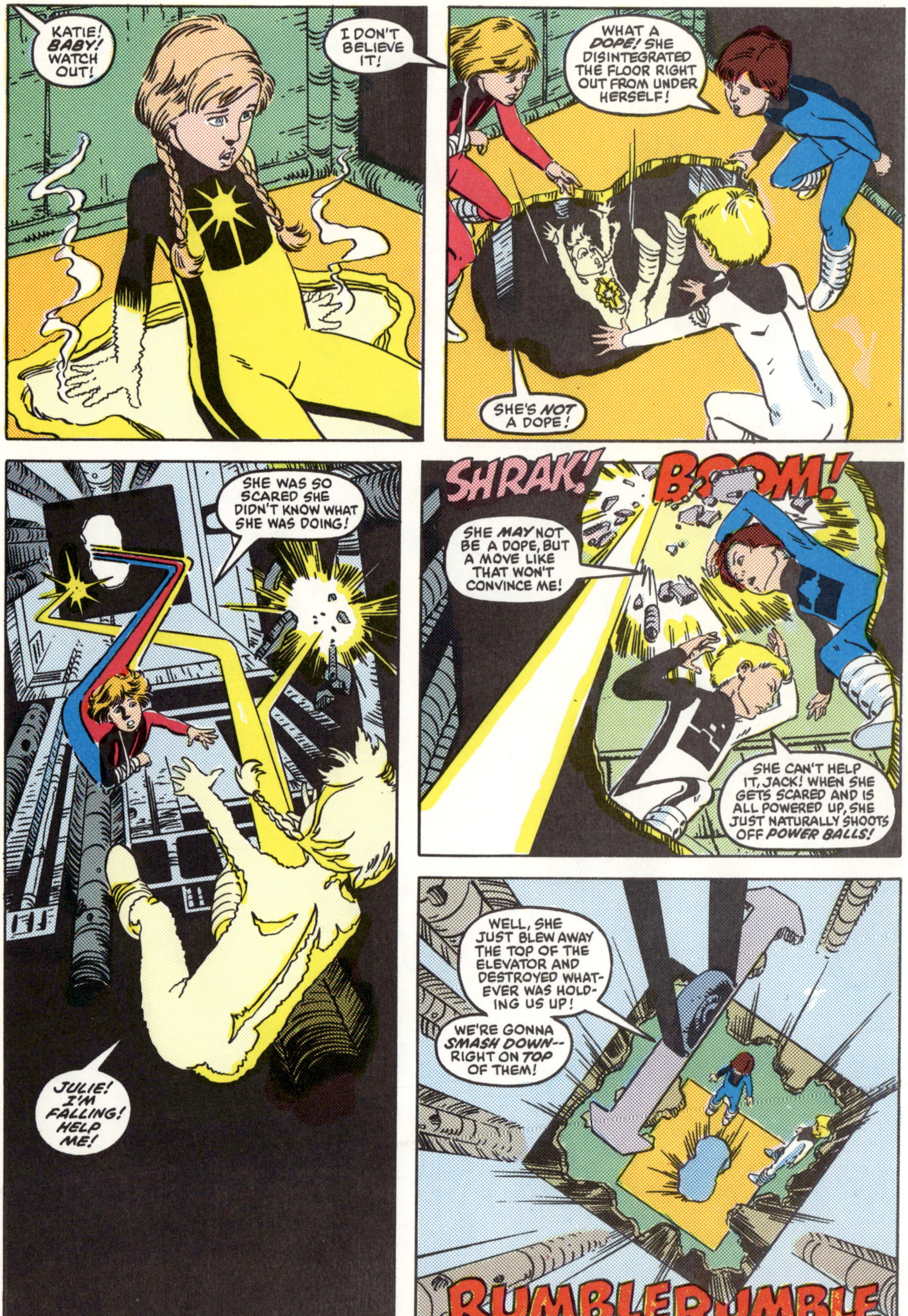
KATIE! BABY! WATCH OUT!
I DON'T BELIEVE IT!
WHAT A DOPE! SHE DISINTEGRATED THE FLOOR RIGHT OUT FROM UNDER HERSELF!
SHE'S NOT A DOPE!
SHE WAS SO SCARED SHE DIDN'T KNOW WHAT SHE WAS DOING!
JULIE! I'M FALLING! HELP ME!
SHRAK!
BOOM!
SHE MAY NOT BE A DOPE, BUT A MOVE LIKE THAT WON'T CONVINCE ME!
SHE CAN'T HELP IT, JACK! WHEN SHE GETS SCARED AND IS ALL POWERED UP, SHE JUST NATURALLY SHOOTS OFF POWER BALLS!
WELL, SHE JUST BLEW AWAY THE TOP OF THE ELEVATOR AND DESTROYED WHAT-EVER WAS HOLD-ING US UP!
WE'RE GONNA SMASH DOWN-- RIGHT ON TOP OF THEM!
RUMBLERUMBLE

RUMBLERUMBLE
OH, THANK HEAVENS!
JULIE! GET OUT OF THE WAY!
OH NO! THE ELEVATOR!
I MADE A HOLE IN THE WALL, TOO!
I SEE IT, BUT WE'LL NEVER REACH IT IN TIME!
WHILE ABOVE...
WE'VE GOT TO STOP THIS THING!
MY GEE POWER'LL CANCEL ITS GRAVITY... BUT--
BUT IT'S GOT LOTS OF MASS AND MOMENTUM! IT JUST KEEPS FALLING!
IT WORKED ...SLOWED IT DOWN A LITTLE!
RUMBLERUMBLE
JULIE! MOVE! HURRY!
RUMBLERUMBLE
CRASH!

MEANWHILE...
YES, QUEEN MOTHER! THE POWER HATCHLINGS HAVE ESCAPED. OBSERVE THE DAMAGE THEY DID TO THE CONTROL ROOM!
SHOULD WE NOT AVOID RENDEZVOUS TILL THEY ARE RECAPTURED? THEY MAY PRESENT A DANGER TO THE MOTHERSHIP ITSELF!
I OBSERVE THAT THEY ARE EVEN BETTER WEAPONS THAN YOU PROMISED. PERHAPS EVEN AS USEFUL AS THE ANNIHILATOR ITSELF!
THEY MUST NOT BE DAMAGED. AND THEY MUST NOT ESCAPE!
BUT QUEEN MOTHER! NOTHING WILL RESTRAIN THEM!
NONSENSE, CAPTAIN! YOU DISPLEASE ME!
I SUGGEST A STABILIZER BEAM! IF IT CAN HOLD A SMARTSHIP POWERLESS...
...IT SHOULD EASILY CONFINE A FEW SMALL HUMANS, EVEN ONES WITH SORCEROUS POWERS.
WHILE ELSEWHERE...
THE GIRLS GOT AWAY ...RIGHT?
I THINK!
LOOK! KATIE'S TOOTH! I--
ALEX! JACK!
WATCH OUT!
ZZZTTTZZZ
THE STABILIZER BEAM IS SUCCESSFUL! THE BOY CHILDREN ARE OURS!

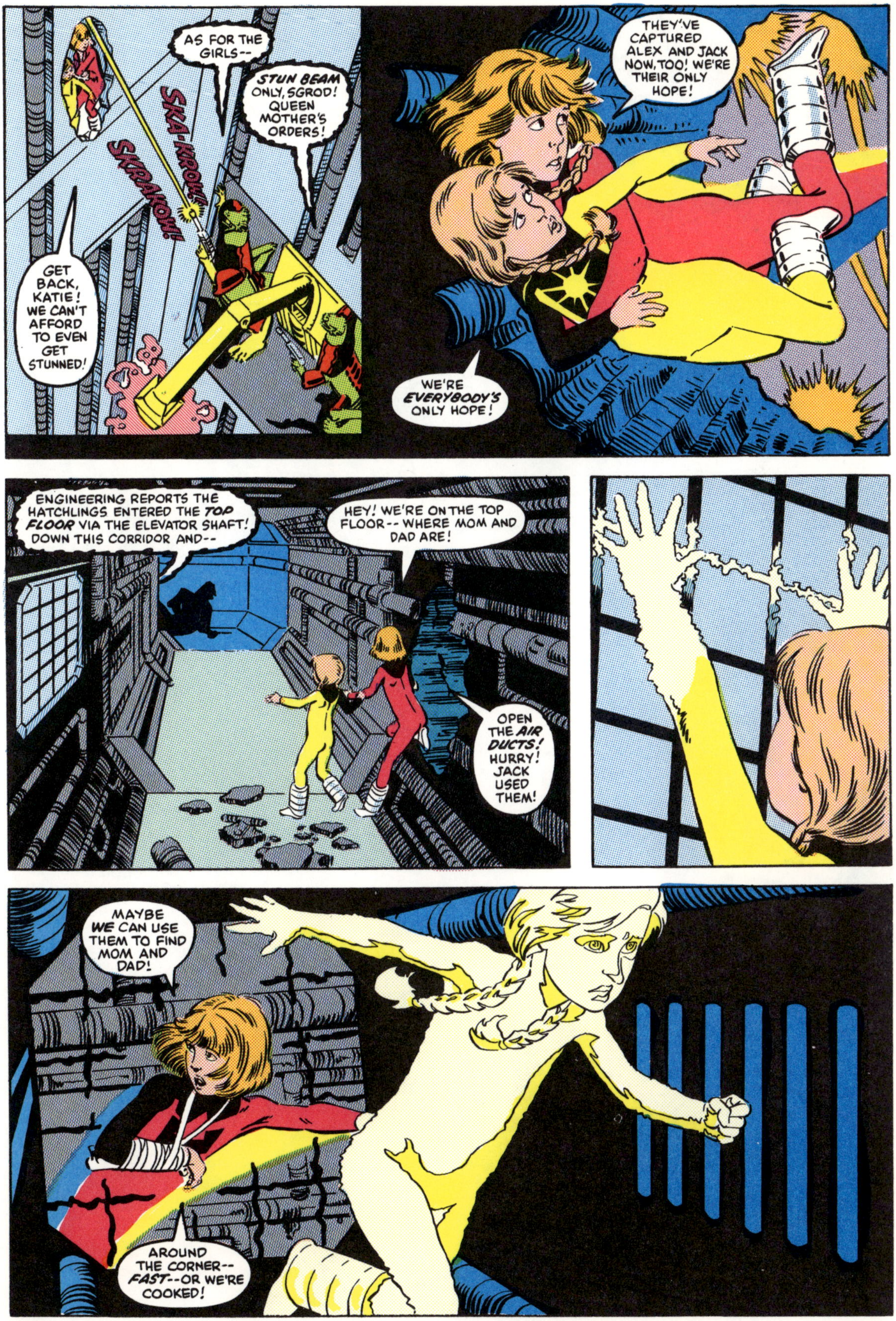
AS FOR THE GIRLS--
STUN BEAM ONLY, SGROD! QUEEN MOTHER'S ORDERS!
SKA-KROOM!
SKRAKOW!
GET BACK, KATIE! WE CAN'T AFFORD TO EVEN GET STUNNED!
THEY'VE CAPTURED ALEX AND JACK NOW, TOO! WE'RE THEIR ONLY HOPE!
WE'RE EVERYBODY'S ONLY HOPE!
ENGINEERING REPORTS THE HATCHLINGS ENTERED THE TOP FLOOR VIA THE ELEVATOR SHAFT! DOWN THIS CORRIDOR AND--
HEY! WE'RE ON THE TOP FLOOR-- WHERE MOM AND DAD ARE!
OPEN THE AIR DUCTS! HURRY! JACK USED THEM!
MAYBE WE CAN USE THEM TO FIND MOM AND DAD!
AROUND THE CORNER-- FAST--OR WE'RE COOKED!

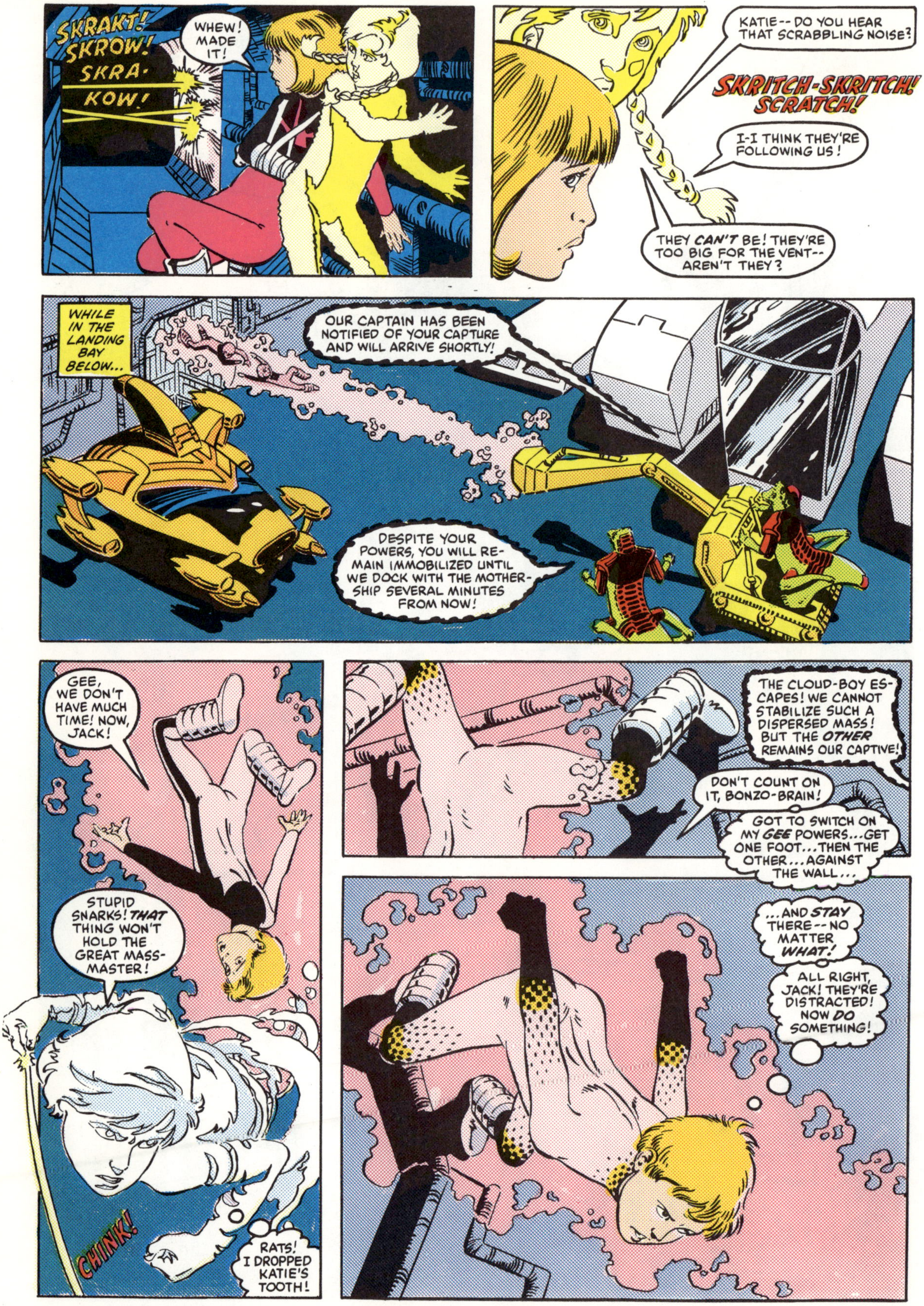
SKRAKT! SKROW! SKRA-KOW!
WHEW! MADE IT!
KATIE--DO YOU HEAR THAT SCRABBLING NOISE?
SKRITCH-SKRITCH! SCRATCH!
I-I THINK THEY'RE FOLLOWING US!
THEY CAN'T BE! THEY'RE TOO BIG FOR THE VENT--AREN'T THEY?
WHILE IN THE LANDING BAY BELOW...
OUR CAPTAIN HAS BEEN NOTIFIED OF YOUR CAPTURE AND WILL ARRIVE SHORTLY!
DESPITE YOUR POWERS, YOU WILL REMAIN IMMOBILIZED UNTIL WE DOCK WITH THE MOTHER-SHIP SEVERAL MINUTES FROM NOW!
GEE, WE DON'T HAVE MUCH TIME! NOW, JACK!
STUPID SNARKS! THAT THING WON'T HOLD THE GREAT MASS-MASTER!
CHINK!
RATS! I DROPPED KATIE'S TOOTH!
THE CLOUD-BOY ESCAPES! WE CANNOT STABILIZE SUCH A DISPERSED MASS! BUT THE OTHER REMAINS OUR CAPTIVE!
DON'T COUNT ON IT, BONZO-BRAIN!
GOT TO SWITCH ON MY GEE POWERS...GET ONE FOOT...THEN THE OTHER...AGAINST THE WALL...
...AND STAY THERE--NO MATTER WHAT!
ALL RIGHT, JACK! THEY'RE DISTRACTED! NOW DO SOMETHING!

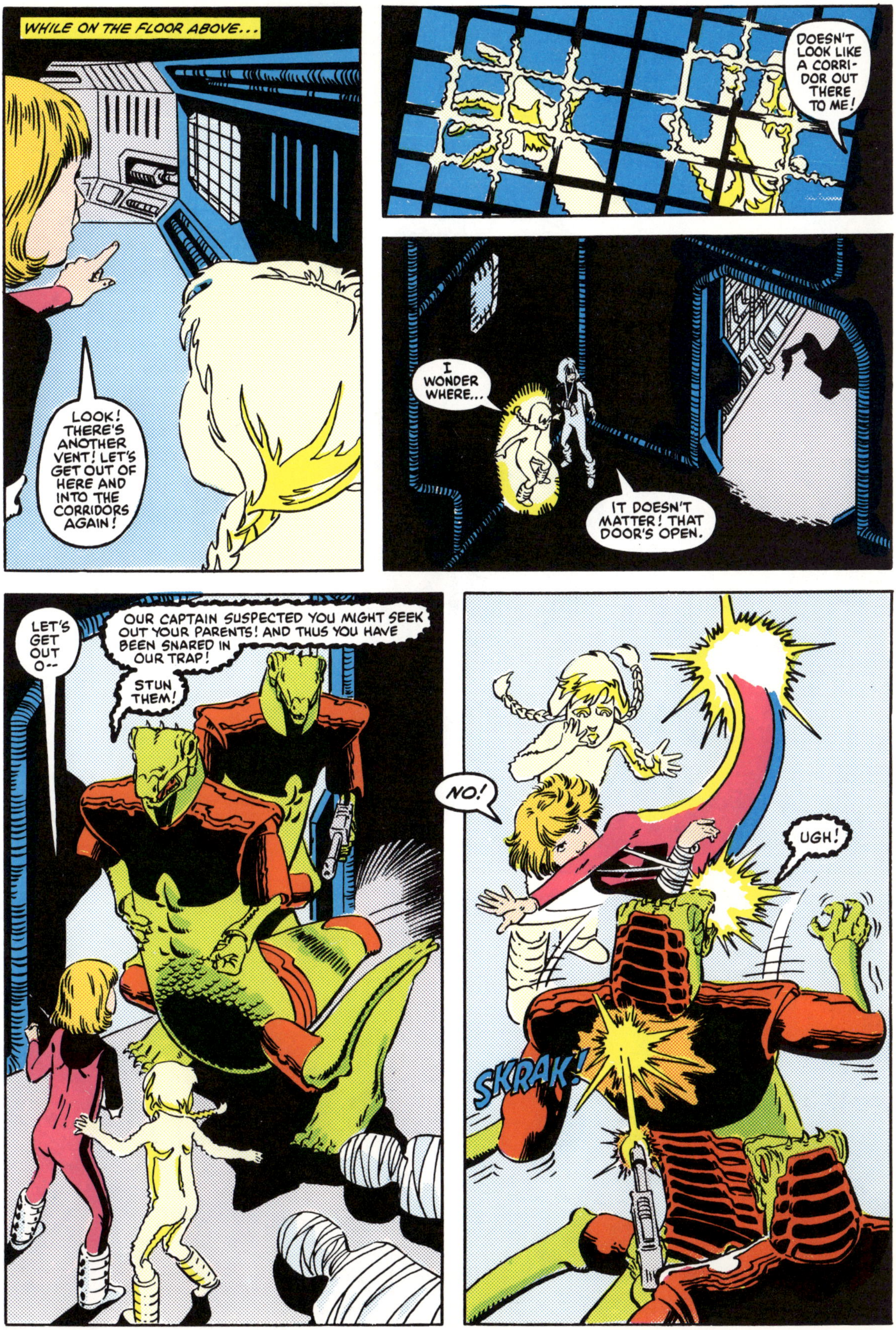
WHILE ON THE FLOOR ABOVE...
LOOK! THERE'S ANOTHER VENT! LET'S GET OUT OF HERE AND INTO THE CORRIDORS AGAIN!
DOESN'T LOOK LIKE A CORRIDOR OUT THERE TO ME!
I WONDER WHERE...
IT DOESN'T MATTER! THAT DOOR'S OPEN.
LET'S GET OUT O--
OUR CAPTAIN SUSPECTED YOU MIGHT SEEK OUT YOUR PARENTS! AND THUS YOU HAVE BEEN SNARED IN OUR TRAP!
STUN THEM!
NO!
UGH!
SKRAK!

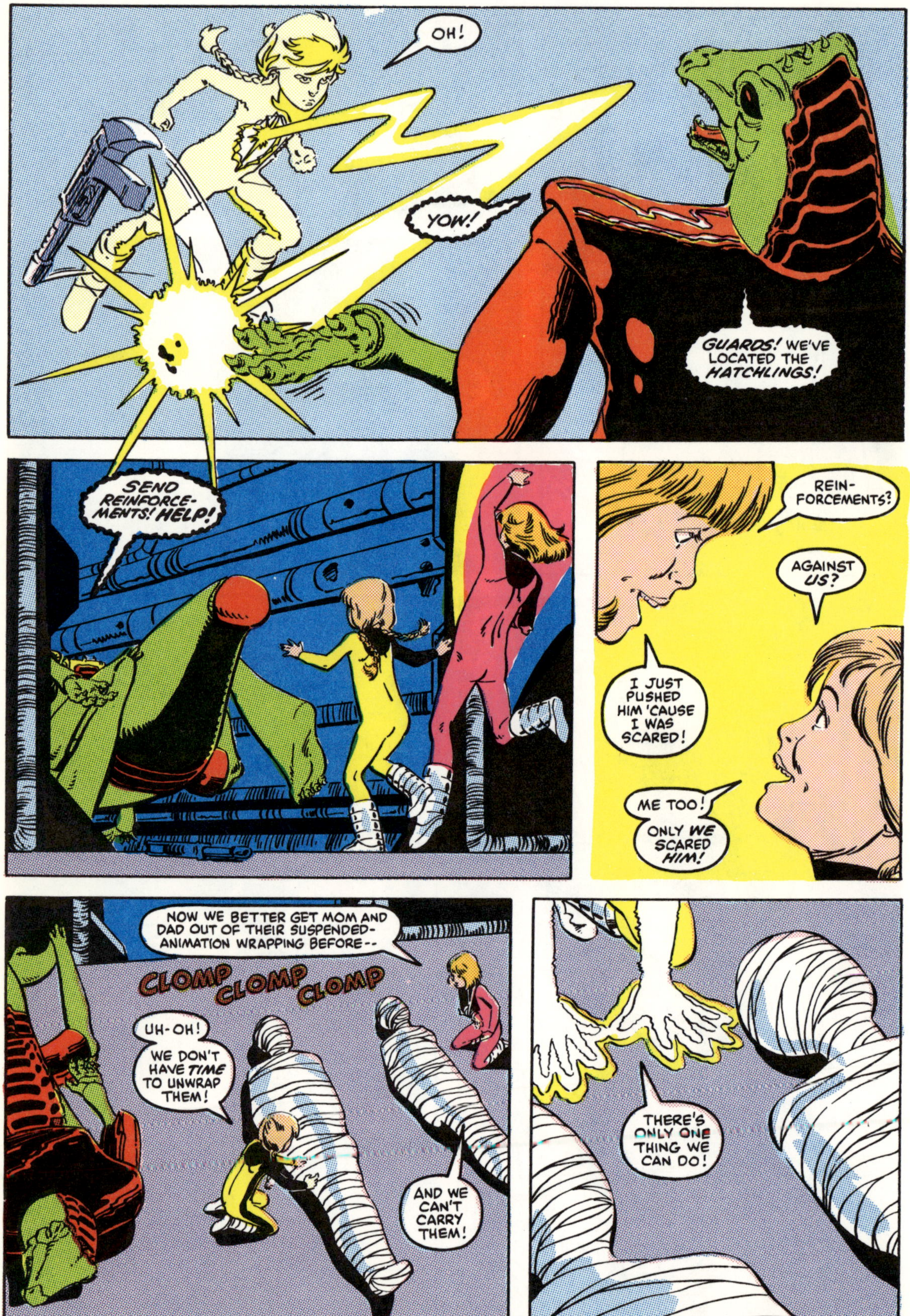
OH!
YOW!
GUARDS! WE'VE LOCATED THE HATCHLINGS!
SEND REINFORCE-MENTS! HELP!
REIN-FORCEMENTS?
AGAINST US?
I JUST PUSHED HIM 'CAUSE I WAS SCARED!
ME TOO!
ONLY WE SCARED HIM!
NOW WE BETTER GET MOM AND DAD OUT OF THEIR SUSPENDED-ANIMATION WRAPPING BEFORE--
CLOMP CLOMP CLOMP
UH-OH!
WE DON'T HAVE TIME TO UNWRAP THEM!
AND WE CAN'T CARRY THEM!
THERE'S ONLY ONE THING WE CAN DO!

MEANWHILE, BELOW...
INCREASE THE PULL OF THE STABILIZER BEAM!
ANY MORE FORCE...
...AND THE WALL WILL COME WITH--
UGH!
THUNK!
YOU'RE FREE, ALEX...
NOW GET FRIDAY LOOSE! THIS THING'S REALLY EASY TO OPERATE!
BUT THEY'RE NOT!
THAT ONE, MAYBE, BUT THIS ONE WON'T BUDGE!
WELL IF I CAN'T TURN IT OFF, MAYBE I CAN SMASH IT!
WITH WHAT?
I'LL DE-GRAVITIZE THAT SNARK FLIER...
...AND DROP IT FROM THE CEILING! IT SHOULD BE HEAVY ENOUGH!
CRASH!
THANK YOU, ALEX! THAT WORKED VERY NICE-LY!

WHAT THE--?
I MIGHTA KNOWN!
ALEX! YOU'RE OKAY! THANK HEAVENS!
WE THOUGHT WE'D HAVE TO RESCUE YOU, TOO! WE'VE GOT MOM AND DAD! HELP US GET THEM DOWN TO FRIDAY!
AND HURRY! THE SNARKS'LL BE HERE ANY SECOND!
SECONDS LATER...
SKRAKT!
YOU FLY PRETTY FAST, JULIE, BUT I DON'T KNOW IF IT'S FAST ENOUGH TO DODGE LASER BLASTS!
YEAH! I'M GLAD I DON'T HAVE TO TEST IT OUT!
SKROW!
WITH OLD MASS-MASTER FOGGING UP THE JOINT, THEY'RE JUST FIRING BLIND ANYHOW!
BUT THEY'RE STILL COMING TOO CLOSE FOR COMFORT! BETTER GET MOM AND DAD INSIDE-- NOW!
SKRAKOW!
MY THOUGHT PRECISELY!
SHRAK!
I DON'T KNOW WHY I'M RISKING MY LIFE OVER THE BRAT'S TOOTH! SOMETIMES I AMAZE EVEN MYSELF!
ALL RIGHT, JACK! WE'RE IN FRIDAY! YOU CAN QUIT MAKING FOG NOW!
JACK? JACK!!!
WHAT ARE YOU GOING SOLID OUTSIDE FOR? YOU'LL BE SHOT!
GET IN HERE!
TAKE IT EASY! MASS-MASTER HAS EVERYTHING UNDER CONTROL!
IF ONLY I DID, JACK!

WHAT DO YOU MEAN, FRIDAY?
PROBLEMS!
IN ABOUT A MINUTE, THE MOTHERSHIP WILL SWALLOW US! MY WEAPONS ARE USELESS AGAINST HER!
COULD YOU OUTRUN HER?
PERHAPS... BUT WE ARE TRAPPED INSIDE!
KATIE, YOU SEE THOSE DOORS?
CAN YOU CONCENTRATE REALLY HARD AND BLOW A HOLE IN THEM?
A GIANT ONE-- BIG ENOUGH FOR FRIDAY TO FLY THROUGH!
OKAY! I'LL TRY!
GET A STABILIZER BEAM BACK ON THAT SMARTSHIP!
IF THEY ESCAPE, THE QUEEN MOTHER WILL HAVE OUR HIDES!
THE LAUNCH DOOR REMAINS SHUT! HOW CAN THEY ESCAPE?
HERE GOES--
BOOM
KATIE! YOU DID IT! I CAN'T BELIEVE IT!
THE HULL IS BREACHED!
EXPLOSIVE DECOMPRESSION!
WE'LL BE SUCKED INTO SPACE!

SHUT THE EMERGENCY SHIELD DO-- URK!
CRAKK
SLAM!
MAY THE QUEEN MOTHER TAKE THEM AND --UGH!
CRASH!
GET A TRACTOR BEAM ON THE SMARTSHIP!
LAUNCH FIGHTERS! IT'S ESCAPING!
OH NO! WHAT'S THAT?
A TRACTOR BEAM, JULIE. LIKE THE KIND THAT GRABBED FRIDAY BACK ON EARTH!
BUT THIS ONE IS STRONGER... MUCH STRONGER! ALREADY WE ARE BEING DRAWN BACK TOWARD THE MOTHERSHIP!
I AM... UNABLE TO RESIST... SUCH FORCE...
OH NO! WHAT'LL WE DO?
UH... LISTEN, KATIE... BEFORE THEY TAKE US, I JUST WANT YOU TO KNOW THAT I LIED... ABOUT THE TOOTH FAIRY AND ALL.
THERE REALLY IS ONE!
THAT'S OKAY, JACK! IT DOESN'T MATTER NOW! I LOST MY TOOTH ANYWAY!
NO YOU HAVEN'T!
OH... JACK!

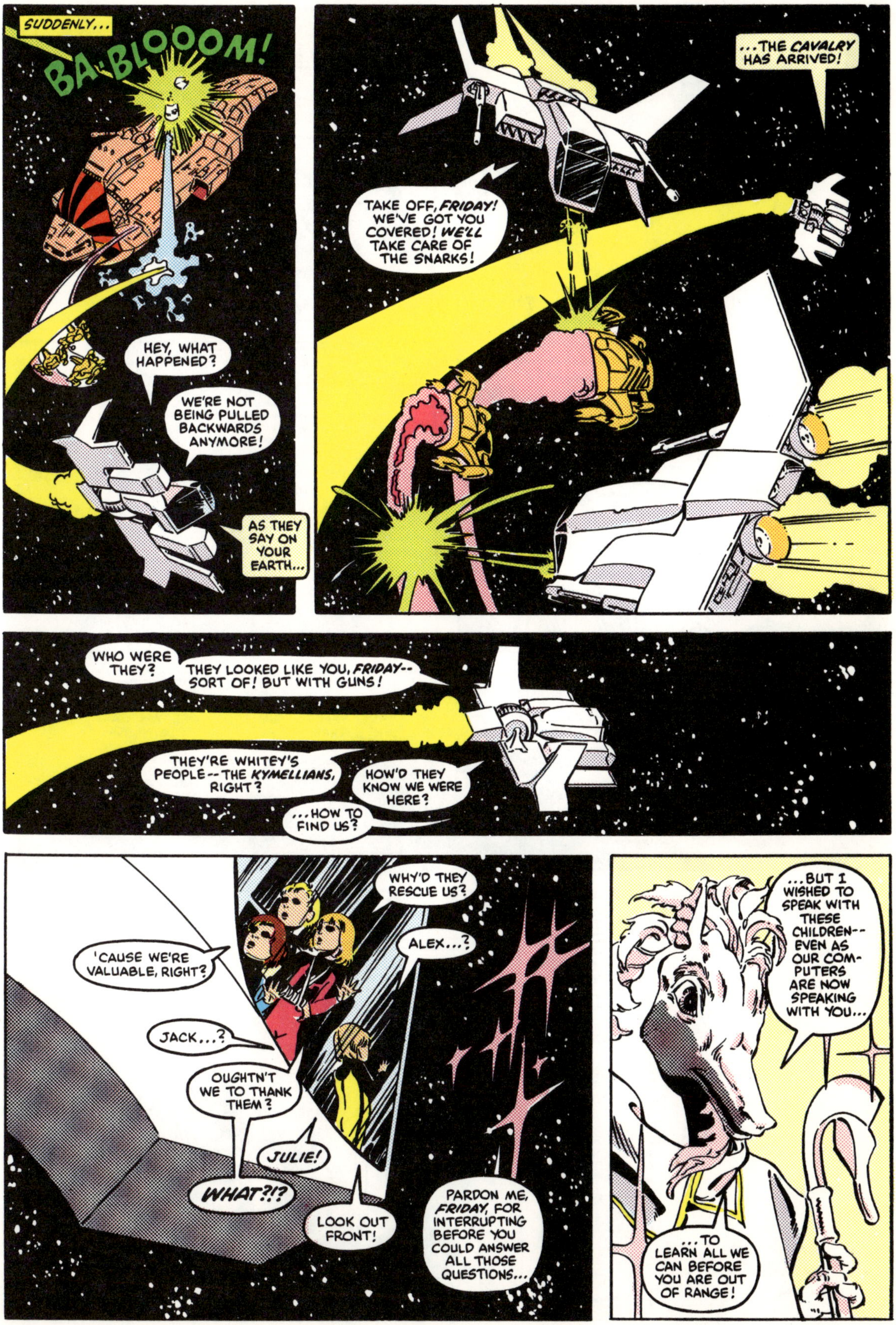
SUDDENLY...
BA-BLOOOM!
HEY, WHAT HAPPENED?
WE'RE NOT BEING PULLED BACKWARDS ANYMORE!
AS THEY SAY ON YOUR EARTH...
...THE CAVALRY HAS ARRIVED!
TAKE OFF, FRIDAY! WE'VE GOT YOU COVERED! WE'LL TAKE CARE OF THE SNARKS!
WHO WERE THEY?
THEY LOOKED LIKE YOU, FRIDAY-- SORT OF! BUT WITH GUNS!
THEY'RE WHITEY'S PEOPLE -- THE KYMELLIANS, RIGHT?
HOW'D THEY KNOW WE WERE HERE?
...HOW TO FIND US?
WHY'D THEY RESCUE US?
ALEX...?
'CAUSE WE'RE VALUABLE, RIGHT?
JACK...?
OUGHTN'T WE TO THANK THEM?
JULIE!
WHAT?!?
LOOK OUT FRONT!
PARDON ME, FRIDAY, FOR INTERRUPTING BEFORE YOU COULD ANSWER ALL THOSE QUESTIONS...
...BUT I WISHED TO SPEAK WITH THESE CHILDREN-- EVEN AS OUR COMPUTERS ARE NOW SPEAKING WITH YOU...
...TO LEARN ALL WE CAN BEFORE YOU ARE OUT OF RANGE!

WHO ARE YOU?
I AM BYREL, A KYMELLIAN TRUTH-SIFTER, AND I AM HERE TO UNDERSTAND, IF POSSIBLE, THE TRULY UN-PRECEDENTED THING THAT AELFYRE WHITEMANE DID!
FOR, UPON HIS DEATH, HE TRANSFERRED HIS POWERS TO ...STRANGERS.
THAT'S BECAUSE HE DIDN'T WANT OUR WORLD TO BE DESTROYED BY THE ANNIHILATOR OUR DAD INVENTED!
HE SAID OUR BOOKS WERE A... A GALACTIC TREASURE AND, BECAUSE OF THEM, THE EARTH SHOULD BE SAVED!
SO HE GAVE US HIS POWERS AND TOLD US TO SAVE IT, AND WE FELT RESPONSIBLE BECAUSE OF DAD'S INVENTION...
...HE DIDN'T MAKE IT TO DESTROY THE WORLD, BUT IT WOULD HAVE ANYWAY! SO WE SMASHED IT!
AND THUS YOU SAVED YOUR WORLD!
AND WHEN THE SNARKS KIDNAPPED YOUR PARENTS AND FRIDAY--YOU RESCUED THEM... ALMOST DESTROYING THE SNARK'S CRUISER IN THE PROCESS!
YOU HAVE SHOWN DETERMINATION, HONOR AND COURAGE BEYOND YOUR YEARS... QUALITIES MORE IMPORTANT THAN THE POWERS WHITEY GAVE YOU!
MY PEOPLE ARE PLEASED BY HIS ACTION--AND YOURS!
WHITEY SAID HE WASN'T ALLOWED TO INTERFERE WITH EARTH... EVEN IF WE WERE READY TO ACCI-DENTALLY BLOW OURSELVES UP!
THAT IS TRUE, JACK... BUT THE SNARKS AT-TACKED YOU IN DEFIANCE OF GALACTIC LAW--AND THUS CREATED AN INTER-GALACTIC INCIDENT!
AND WHITEY CHOSE A MOST--UNUSUAL WAY OF DEALING WITH IT!
SO IF THE SNARKS HADN'T GONE AFTER MOM AND DAD, WHITEY WOULDN'T HAVE GIVEN US HIS POWERS AND EARTH WOULD HAVE BEEN DESTROYED!
GEE! MAYBE WE SHOULD TURN AROUND AND THANK THEM!
BITE YOUR TONGUE, BEAN-BRAIN!

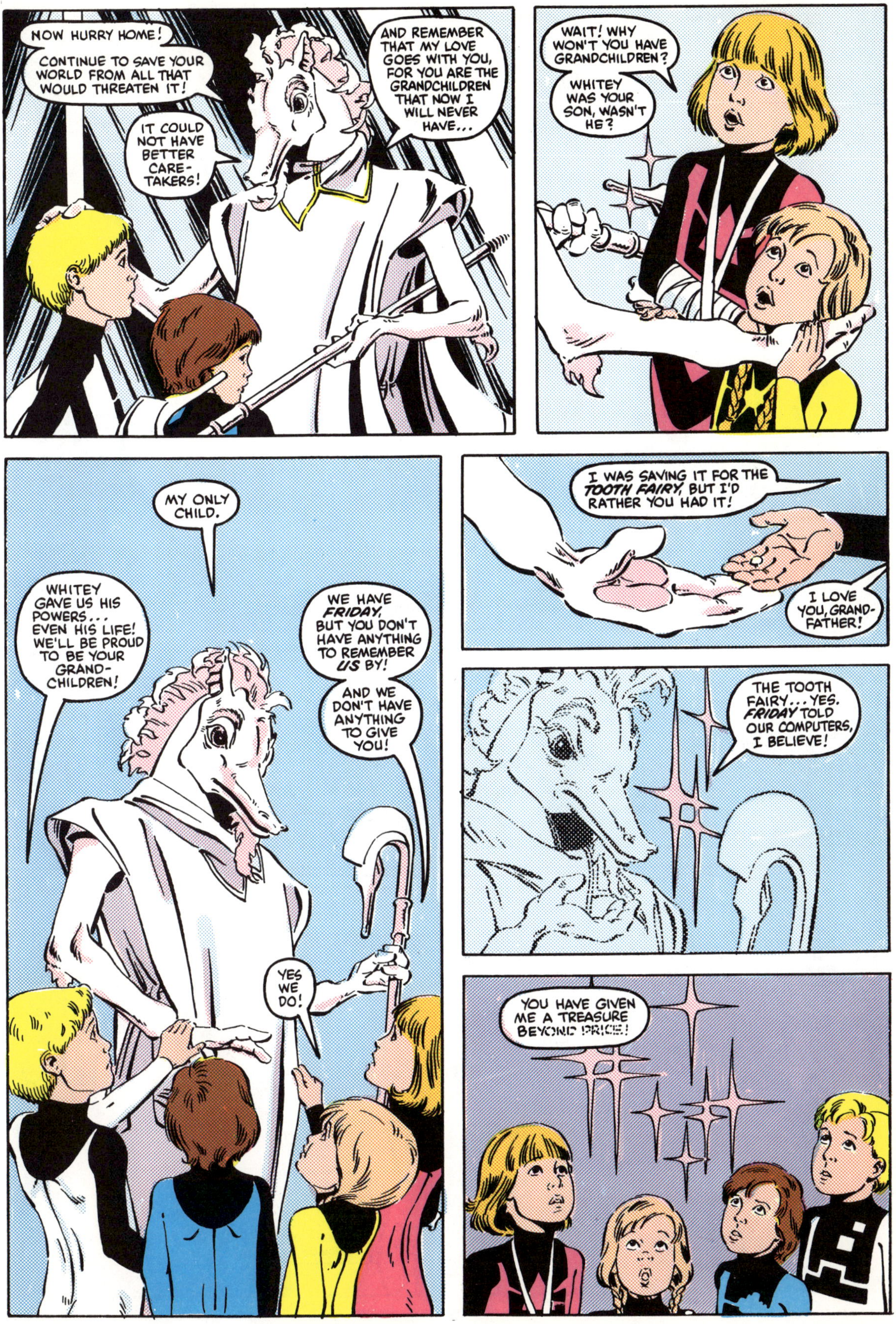
NOW HURRY HOME!
CONTINUE TO SAVE YOUR WORLD FROM ALL THAT WOULD THREATEN IT!
IT COULD NOT HAVE BETTER CARE-TAKERS!
AND REMEMBER THAT MY LOVE GOES WITH YOU, FOR YOU ARE THE GRANDCHILDREN THAT NOW I WILL NEVER HAVE...
WAIT! WHY WON'T YOU HAVE GRANDCHILDREN?
WHITEY WAS YOUR SON, WASN'T HE?
MY ONLY CHILD.
WHITEY GAVE US HIS POWERS... EVEN HIS LIFE! WE'LL BE PROUD TO BE YOUR GRAND-CHILDREN!
WE HAVE FRIDAY, BUT YOU DON'T HAVE ANYTHING TO REMEMBER US BY!
AND WE DON'T HAVE ANYTHING TO GIVE YOU!
YES WE DO!
I WAS SAVING IT FOR THE TOOTH FAIRY, BUT I'D RATHER YOU HAD IT!
I LOVE YOU, GRAND-FATHER!
THE TOOTH FAIRY... YES. FRIDAY TOLD OUR COMPUTERS, I BELIEVE!
YOU HAVE GIVEN ME A TREASURE BEYOND PRICE!

LATER...
FRIDAY...
YES, JACK?
IT JUST DOESN'T SEEM RIGHT NOT TO UNWRAP MOM AND DAD TILL WE GET HOME!
AWAKE, THEY WOULD CONSUME VALUABLE FOOD AND AIR. AND THEY WOULD WORRY! IT IS BETTER TO WAIT!
YEAH! MOM WOULD FUSS ABOUT JULIE'S ARM AND DAD WOULD LECTURE US ABOUT DOING DANGEROUS THINGS!
I GUESS YOU'RE RIGHT...BUT THEY SURE WOULD LOVE THE VIEW! AND SPEAKING OF FOOD... I'M STARVED!
ME TOO! IS THERE ANYTHING TO EAT?
ONLY THIS! IT'S QUITE NUTRITIOUS ...AND WHITEY LIKED IT A LOT!
IT'S BLUE...
BUT IF WHITEY LIKED IT, IT'S GOOD ENOUGH FOR ME!
HEY, WHAT'S THAT?
CLINK!
IT WAS UNDER MY PILLOW! IT'S FROM THE TOOTH FAIRY! IT HAS TO BE! BUT HOW'D SHE FIND ME HERE?
HOLY COW! IT HAS GRANDFATHER'S PICTURE ON IT! SHE NEVER GAVE ME ONE EVEN NEAR THAT GOOD!
THAT'S 'CAUSE YOU NEVER BELIEVED IN HER!
AND LIGHTYEARS AWAY, A KYMELLIAN SORCERER SMILES!

Louise Simonson

was born in Atlanta, Georgia and spent most of her childhood with her nose in a book or an enthralling fantasy game with her sisters and neighborhood friends. After attending Georgia State College, she came to New York where she worked first in circulation, then in advertising-promotion for a major magazine publisher. She was senior editor at the now-defunct Warren Publishing before coming to Marvel Comics, where she edited X-Men and Star Wars among other titles. She is currently the writer on hot Marvel titles X-Factor and New Mutants. And "Weezie" (that's really her nickname) still has her nose in a book, whenever she hasn't got her fingers on the word-processor keyboard.

June Brigman

was also born in Atlanta and has been drawing since she was old enough to hold a pencil. She didn't read comics as a child; in fact, she was 19 before she seriously looked at a comic. She has studied art at the University of Georgia and Georgia State University, but her illustrations are solidly based on real-life observation skills she developed over a summer as a pastel portrait artist at Six Flags Over Georgia. When June showed her samples on a trip into the Marvel offices in New York, Louise Simonson was "blown away by their quality," and the rest is history. June's other penciling credits include Alpha Flight and Strange Tales.

Bob Wiacek

was born in Manhattan, and now lives Upstate with his wife Ann. His ill-spent youth included hours of monster movies, old Marvel monster comics, and drawing. The influences of Jack Kirby and Steve Ditko led him to the School of Visual Arts in New York, where he was taught by Will Eisner and Harvey Kurtzman. He apprenticed at Neal Adam's Continuity Associates, and in no time was inking DC's Legion of Super Heroes. His first Marvel assignment, "Guardians of the Galaxy" in Marvel Presents, launched a career that has made him one of comics' most sought-after inkers. His long list of credits include Star Wars, Man-Thing, X-Men and X-Factor.

Caricatures by Walt Simonson

Our First Four Adventures